...had ninety minutes, and I required all of them to win this little battle of wills.

Uncertainty lined her shoulders, confusing me. As a siren, nudity shouldn't bother her in the slightest. She spent most of her life naked in the waves. Although, oddly, I couldn't scent the ocean on her.

When was the last time you went for a swim? I wanted to ask. Most of her kind couldn't stand to be on land for too long. They craved the sea, much as I did.

"Is there a problem?" I demanded.

"N-no. I'm just… Never mind." The tinge of fear in her tone confused me even more.

I almost fell for the act, almost asked her to finish the original sentence, but her spine straightened as if she'd made some sort of decision.

She lifted her nimble fingers to the straps of her dress to drag them over her shoulders to her lightly toned arms and then downward to expose her beautiful breasts. I'd seen them once upon a time, in the waves of our home. But I'd never been given the opportunity to touch them.

That would change tonight.

I would possess every inch of her. Every moan. Every breath. She wouldn't inhale without smelling the sea and my underlying power. And once she was addicted, I'd shatter her. Leave her to the depths of the ocean in despair, where she belonged.

No one defied me and got away with it.

Not even someone as gorgeous and alluring as my Kailiani.

Rotanev

A Poseidon Story

USA Today Bestselling Author

Lexi C. Foss

Rotanev

Copyright © 2021 Lexi C. Foss

Editing by: Outthink Editing, LLC

Proofreading by: Jean Bachen & Katie Schmahl

Cover Design: Joolz & Jarling Book Covers

Cover Photography: Wander Aguiar

Cover Models: Zack & Dina

Interior Photos of Sounion: Captured by Lexi C. Foss in 2014

Print Edition

ISBN: 978-1-954183-72-8

❀ Created with Vellum

To the Archaeological Site of Sounion, for the inspiration and the memories

Rotanev

A POSEIDON STORY

A Note from Lexi

Dear Reader,

I love Poseidon. He's my favorite God from mythology, one I've been obsessed with since I was very young. When my Brazilian publisher asked me to write a short story on him for an anthology in Brazil, I jumped at the opportunity. But there was a word limit.

As a result, *Rotanev* is a little different from my usual storytelling. There is a huge world lurking in the background of this tale, one I may explore more of someday but don't have plans to do anytime soon.

You'll also see that I've taken several liberties with mythological contexts, mostly because that's how my brain works. Thus, this tale is very much my own take on Poseidon.

I hope you enjoy Nero and Liani's story. Just be advised, the content is hot. Nero Rotanev is a god, after all. And Liani is his long-lost siren. Their relationship is… intense. And there are also dark undertones and content that might make some readers uncomfortable. But mostly, it's just Nero turning fire into steam with his oceanic touch. ;)

Enjoy!

Hugs,
Lexi

Rotanev

Kailiani Mikos

My life is a mess.
One minute, I'm on my way to graduating, and the next, I find out my mother handed me over as collateral to a loan shark.
Now I'm standing inside a fancy hotel suite in a tiny little dress, auditioning to become an escort for Jasmine Black Incorporated.

That's when I see him. God in a suit. Ocean-blue eyes. Dark, wavy hair. All sensual lines and hard masculinity.
Nero Rotanev.
He sets my blood on fire with a single glance. So when he asks if I will kneel for him, I eagerly agree.

Only something isn't right here.
I feel as though I've known him for eternity.
Except that's impossible, right?

Who are you really, Mister Rotanev?

And why have you chosen me?

Nero Rotanev

Mortals call me Poseidon. Neptune. God.
Kailiani was meant to call me her soul mate. Ah, but my
darling little siren disappeared before I could claim her. And
I've been hunting her ever since.

However, my scouts have finally found her in the Human
Realm.
Hiding among the mortals.
How quaint.

That won't stop me from destroying her. My sweet siren is
going to crawl and beg for my mercy. Oh, but I can't wait to
watch her bleed.

Kailiani will pay for her sins.
And the wrath of the seas will drown her for eternity.

Prepare to kneel, little one.
For no one can outswim me.
Not even a sweet little siren created by the stars.

Author's Note: *Rotanev* is a standalone paranormal
romance featuring a furious Poseidon and his runaway siren.
It's a contemporary tale twisted with mythology and dark
fantasy undertones.

"WE EXIST IN A
WORLD OF REALMS
WHERE EVERY MYTH AND
LEGEND YOU'VE EVER
HEARD IS BASED
ON SOMETHING REAL."

— *Rotanev*

PROLOGUE
Nero Rotanev

"AM I NOT A FAIR GOD?" I asked, yanking on the seaweed restraints securing my prisoner to the beach. "Do I not give my people everything they desire and more?"

Because this miscreant seemed to feel otherwise, what with trying to disturb the maidens protected beneath my waves. They were not to be touched unless they desired it, and this scum of the realm tried to taste the forbidden without permission.

"I... I..."

"You... you...," I mocked, tsking. "I'm bored." Power whirled behind me in the form of two dangerous cyclones, both intent on ripping this poor excuse of a man to shreds.

"My lord." Maheer's voice came from the edge of the

tree line. His golden head reflected the moon in his long, braided strands as he stepped out from beneath the shadow of leaves. "Forgive the interruption, but the Telchines have brought news of the other realms."

I paused the stirring of water energy, allowing it to hang forebodingly over my shoulders, and focused on my second-in-command. "What news?"

He swallowed, his fear poignant and palpable. "It's *her*. They've found her."

"Where?" A single word, underlined with authority.

"Earth."

The cyclones crashed into the shore, taking the prisoner I'd been torturing with them and snapping his neck with an unsatisfying crunch.

Maheer winced at the gruesome display while I sighed, "That was a waste." I could have had so much more fun with him. Alas, it seemed my attentions were required elsewhere. "Are they certain?" Because the last time word of Kailiani's presence reached me, it'd been a false lead. And I was not happy.

"Yes," he replied as I joined him on the dry sand. "I've seen the photos myself, my lord. It's definitely her."

"Photos?" I repeated, intrigued. "And how does my former betrothed look?"

"Beautiful, my lord."

I snorted. "Of course she does. I'll want to review the evidence. If it proves true, reward the Telchines appropriately and tell no one."

He bowed. "Yes, my lord."

"And, Maheer?" I waited until he finally looked at me. "Find me a Realm Dweller. I'll be going after her myself this time."

It'd been a long time since I ventured to the Human Realm.

Poseidon, God of the Sea.

Ah, that'd been a fun era.

Maybe they still worshipped me.

If not, I'd have fun stirring up new trouble while locating the vixen who'd escaped my grasp all those centuries ago.

Swim fast, little one. For I'm coming for you, my darling Kailiani. And I'm bringing the wrath of the seas with me.

LIANI

CHAPTER ONE

THE INVITATION SAT heavy in my hand. Well, technically, it was a business card. But it read like a summons.

An audition, Jasmine Black had called it.

Just showing up guaranteed me one thousand dollars. If I stayed until the end, another thousand. And that was just the reward for mingling. If I was given a job with Jasmine Black Incorporated, also known as JBI, I could make upwards of ten thousand dollars a week.

By becoming a whore.

I flinched at the thought. True, yes. But this was temporary. Once I paid off Corban, I could quit and run far away from New York City.

Just a few weeks.

I could handle that.

It was only my body. I'd endured far worse. Not all pain was physical.

The driver navigated Manhattan, his bodyguard-like presence daunting. JBI had sent him to retrieve me, and aside from an initial greeting, he'd remained stoic and silent. It unsettled my insides, made me question my decision to proceed with tonight. But Veronica—the one who'd recruited me into this mess—promised this agency was legit. Well, as legit as a high-class *escort service* could get.

I saw through the terminology.

I knew what would be expected of me.

No one paid a grand for a date without expecting something in return. And, according to the contract I'd reviewed, some dates required an overnight experience.

Didn't take a genius to figure out what *that* meant.

"We're here, ma'am," the driver announced, pulling up to a stop outside a fancy hotel overlooking Central Park. My invitation would grant me access to the top floor—where the party was located.

"Thank you." I touched the handle just as the door opened for me, another man in a suit with an earpiece standing outside.

"Miss Mikos," he greeted me, holding out his hand. "I'll be escorting you upstairs."

"Oh. Okay." I accepted his help from the car even though I didn't need it. One of tonight's requirements was to leave all personal items at home. As such, I had a key tucked into my thong because my backless dress didn't allow for a bra. And the business card in my hand.

The cool early spring air touched my exposed arms, sending a chill down my spine as the unnamed man beside me accompanied me up the stairs and into the building. He nodded at the doorman and the couples lingering inside, leading us directly to a bank of elevators at the back of the ornately decorated lobby.

"How was the drive?" he asked, his voice warmer than I expected, almost friendly.

"Uneventful," I replied, my throat dry.

The doors opened, and he ushered me inside with a palm against my lower back. As soon as we were alone, he pressed a button and faced me. "Card, please."

I handed it to him.

"This is going to go around your wrist," he said as he produced a cuff-like gold bracelet. He held it out for me. "Hold for a moment."

I did and examined the initials carved into the top—*JBI*.

"The code on your card is tied to your account," he added while keying it into a handheld device. "If someone wishes to purchase time with you, they'll do so by touching their watch to that." He gestured to the cuff. "Clients, including our new ones in attendance tonight, are all trained on the process." He finished typing, then took the bracelet back and scanned it with his phone-sized gadget. "Pretty straightforward."

Sure. For him. I, however, was overwhelmed.

A client can purchase me tonight? That hadn't been explained as part of the audition process. I thought I was just supposed to show up and see how the party went. Then be paid for attending. Not potentially *entertain* someone.

I shivered at the prospect, suddenly very uncertain of my decision to come tonight.

There's no other choice. If you don't get Corban the money…

I shook off the thought, unwilling to think of him tonight. It would only make all of this worse. He already owned my soul. Nothing could hurt more than that. Including selling my body.

"Wrist," the man beside me requested after he finished.

I held it up mutely, uncertain of what to say while he fastened the cuff around my skin. It clicked with a finality that seemed to seal my fate.

"See this button here?" He gestured to the tiny indent on the side of the metal. "Press it if someone steps over the line. Miss Black believes in consensual arrangements, not forced ones." His gray eyes peered down into mine with those words, a kindness lurking in the depths of his irises. "You'll be fine."

Easy for him to say, but I appreciated the vote of confidence anyway. "Thank you."

He nodded and pressed another button on the elevator, sending us upward. "Any final questions?" he asked.

About a million. But "No" was all I said in reply.

"Just mingle, have a good time, and if someone propositions you, negotiate." He winked at that last bit of advice.

The doors opened before I could reply, and his palm found my lower back again, urging me forward into another lobby of sorts. "Liani is here," he said to the petite blonde behind the desk.

"Just in time." She gave me a once-over, her nod signifying she approved of my dress. Considering the agency had sent it for me to wear, she *should* approve.

"Enjoy," my bodyguard-like companion murmured before leaving me in the lobby with the pristinely dressed woman.

She stood with a clipboard and walked around the white desk. "Oliver explained the cuff?"

I nodded. "Yes."

"Perfect. Then all you need to do is enter and socialize.

The party ends at two, but you're free to leave anytime—on your own, or with a client. Just make sure to check out with me before you go." She smiled. "Miss Black will be in touch early next week with results. Just be advised there are twenty of you auditioning and only two available positions on our staff."

My stomach churned. *Twenty candidates? All competing beyond those smoked glass doors? Damn...*

"If you'll just sign this final waiver, I can grant your entry, and the evening may begin."

Another waiver? I thought, accepting the clipboard and pen. I'd already signed my life away to this agency without even being hired. What could this one possibly say?

"It explains how booking works. Feel free to read it over," she said as if hearing my thoughts.

I didn't reply, my eyes too busy absorbing the words.

Rules.

It wasn't an explanation, like she'd claimed, but a list of what I was allowed to do with the clients. Many would want to talk to me, something I wasn't allowed to charge for. They may even indulge in a few touches—also allowed without payment. But if anyone requested alone time in one of the bedrooms or elsewhere, then a negotiation could occur.

Hard limits were to be addressed prior to engaging in any acts.

Key performance objectives were to be mutually agreed upon.

And once the session started, I couldn't stop it unless the client broke a previously negotiated item. Changing objectives or limits during the session was strictly prohibited. While JBI required consent, it did not allow its escorts to function as teases who reneged on certain requests.

Each statement curled in my gut. I'd expected to be

looked at tonight—the dress guaranteed it. But I hadn't anticipated *this*.

Alas, the final stipulations of the document taunted me.

Another one thousand dollars will be deposited once the shift is completed. Failure to stay until the requisite hour forfeits any and all bonuses.

Meaning, if I didn't remain, I'd lose half the money for this audition. And I couldn't afford that. I *needed* those funds. It would serve as a healthy down payment to Corban, a show of good faith that would hopefully be enough.

I had no choice.

I had to sign.

And so I did, another piece of my existence being given away to someone else to manage. It seemed the only part of me I owned these days was my heart.

"Thank you," the woman said, taking the clipboard and pen from me. "Enter through those doors. You're candidate number seventeen, meaning sixteen have already arrived. I suggest you not waste time and get started." Her hazel eyes twinkled, not in a condescending way but in a humored one. "Good luck, sweetheart."

I nodded, my tongue too thick in my mouth to speak. Why had I been among the last to arrive? Because they wanted me to fail? Or because they thought the others needed more time? Why not have us all arrive at once?

Stop thinking and just move, I told myself, my stilettos wobbling as I took a step. I winced and fought the urge to pinch the bridge of my nose.

I can do this.

One night.

Two thousand dollars with the potential for more.

Go in there, smile, and socialize. Maybe you'll meet someone interesting.

I swallowed. The last *interesting* person I met was Corban, and that hadn't ended well.

"Is there a problem, Liani?" the woman asked, picking up on my hesitation.

"No," I managed to say, the sound coming out on an undignified croak. I cleared my throat and tried again. "No, I'm fine. Just considering my strategy."

She chuckled. "I suggest you enter first, then consider. It might help you see what you're up against."

Something told me that would do the exact opposite, but I nodded again and grabbed the handle. A snick of sound indicated she'd hit a button of sorts to unlock the doors. Then I pushed one open and stepped over the threshold.

Wealth and opulence hit me at once, the decorations screaming elegance, from the leather seating to the crystal glasses and the very finely dressed men and women mingling throughout the room. My black gown—the same color as my hair—fit right in, as did the gold cuff glinting in the sensual lighting.

Windows overlooking Manhattan spanned the back wall of the large space, a bar was situated in one corner, and two men in suits stood guarding a hallway to my right.

The bedrooms.

Right.

I went toward the bar instead, needing some liquid courage. There was nothing in the paperwork about not being able to drink. Besides, a glance around showed everyone had alcohol, even the other females wearing gold cuffs like my own.

Of course, all those women were already chatting up men in suits.

Most of the males in this place were old enough to be my father. Not that I'd ever met my sperm donor, but I imagined him to be in his forties or fifties.

The bartender slid a glass of champagne my way. "Compliments of the gentleman at the end," he said, nodding toward a silver-haired man at the edge of the bar.

Well, that didn't take long, I thought, smiling at him as I lifted the glass to my lips. *Too bad you look far too old to provide appropriate entertainment.*

Or maybe that was exactly what I needed.

A man who desired to just… talk.

Hmm.

I started toward him, when a shiver of awareness danced over my skin, causing my focus to shift to the entrance. An eerie hum of energy swam through the air, tickling the hairs along my arms.

And then *he* entered.

A god in an all-black suit.

My lips actually parted because *wow*. This man put all the others in this room—hell, this *city*—to shame. And the way he carried himself as he entered said he knew it, too. He possessed the stature of a person used to others bowing to him in every way.

He owned the suite with each step, drawing several stares to his chiseled features.

Perfection.

I had no better word for it. Everything about him was pure male perfection.

He moved with a purpose toward the bar, ignoring everyone and everything in his path. Including me, as he paused at the stool to my right to order an expensive label of scotch.

I considered stepping backward, or shifting around him to join the elderly man at the end, but my feet refused me. Just as I couldn't stop myself from studying his profile.

Straight nose.

Square jaw.

Eyelashes of the darkest shades.

Thick, nearly black hair.

And eyes the color of the deepest depths of the ocean.

"It's rude to stare," he murmured, smirking at me. "Although, I suppose I can forgive the boldness if you promise to kneel for me later."

Warmth crept up my neck at his words, as well as being caught in the act of gawking. An apology slipped to the tip of my tongue, only to be beat out by a witty reply: "I can think of worse punishments than having to kneel for you." *What. The. Hell. Was. That?*

His eyebrow lifted, his lips curling into a devastating grin. "Perhaps we'll explore those, too." He fully faced me, his elbow resting on the bar. "In fact, I'm certain we will."

The promise underlining his tone sent a bolt of lust straight to my gut. Confidence was an aphrodisiac, and this man redefined the meaning of the word.

"Liani," I said, holding out my hand.

A flicker of surprise entered his irises, as if he hadn't expected me to introduce myself. Was that against the code? Because no one told me not to say my name.

"Liani," he repeated as if tasting the word. "That's not your full name."

An odd thing for him to say, but he wasn't wrong. "No, it's not. It's short for Kailiani."

Another wave of surprise loosened his features, as if he'd not expected such a name.

"It's Hawaiian," I explained awkwardly.

He tilted his head to the side. "Is it? Because I swear it's the name of a siren."

"From mythology?" I wondered out loud, thinking back on some of my college courses. "I'm not sure. I've not heard of a Kailiani. I just know it stems from Kailani in Hawaiian, which does mean 'the sea' or 'the sky.'" *Why am I jabbering about this?* This was not seductive conversation and had to be the wrong way to persuade a man into an *arrangement*.

"Fascinating," he replied. "I'm Nero. Greek for 'water.' "

My lips curled. "Some might say we're meant to meet, then."

"Many would, yes." The bartender returned with his drink, but Nero didn't touch it, his attention solely on me as his gaze danced over every inch of my dress. "How old are you, Kailiani?"

I almost told him I preferred to be called Liani, but the way he spoke my name made it impossible to voice a correction. Because it sounded so perfect from his lips, so *right*. And wasn't that strange? I barely knew this man, yet I could swear I'd heard him call me Kailiani before in my dreams.

He looked at me expectantly, reminding me that he'd just asked me something.

My age.

Right.

"Twenty-two," I replied honestly.

Then wondered if I was supposed to be giving these details about myself. I knew my home address was a secret to be kept from all clients for security purposes. Not that any of them couldn't find me if they wanted to. If these wealthy men wanted to locate someone, their bank accounts could afford them whatever information they desired.

"So young," Nero mused, a glimmer in his eyes.

I studied his crisp suit, athletic physique, and handsome face. "You can't be that much older. Maybe thirty."

His lips quirked up on one side. "Oh, I am much older than thirty."

"Somehow, I doubt that," I replied, taking his flirtatious bait. "Thirty-five at most."

He chuckled. "I'm beginning to think you actually don't know."

"Should I?" Was he someone famous that I should recognize? Because I sucked at the who's-who socialite game. I was too busy surviving to memorize bachelor profiles. Assuming all the men here were even single.

Maybe I should be researching some of these men. The last thing I wanted to do was get in the middle of a troubled marriage.

Nero finally took a sip of his scotch, his gorgeous eyes regarding me the entire time. Then he set it to the side with a finality. "Mmm, all right, little one. I'll play, but only because you have me intrigued. An hour ought to be enough to break you, yes?"

My eyebrows rose. "Break me?" I wasn't sure I liked the sound of that. And yet, the devious twinkle in his gaze had me wanting to say yes anyway.

He leaned in, his lips brushing my ear. "You did agree to kneel for me, did you not?"

My thighs clenched in response. "Oh. I, yes. Yes, I did."

"Then I want an hour," he replied, his palm falling to my hip. "Alone."

I inhaled sharply, his scent—crisp as an ocean breeze—overwhelming my ability to think. There was something I should do, words I needed to say. But as he drew back to stare down at me through his hypnotic irises, all I could do was nod.

Everything about him struck me as a take-charge kind of man. He required submission, and some ingrained part of me readily gave it.

"Is that a yes?" he asked, a hint of amusement in his tone.

"Yes," I whispered, unable to utter another sound. I couldn't believe I was actually agreeing to this, to an hour alone with a man I didn't know. But this entire week had been about doing things outside my comfort zone, from the interview to the mostly nude photos I took afterward to showing up tonight for this audition.

It was exciting. Terrifying. Thrilling. Intoxicating.

Because even without the guarantee of payment for tonight, I'd be tempted to follow this man. He was *that* charismatic that the idea of a one-night stand more than appealed to me. And I'd never done anything of the sort.

Actually, my experience bordered on pathetic. Which evoked a whole flurry of concerns.

What if I don't satisfy him?

What if I mess this up?

What if he finds out I'm—

His hand lifted and curled around the back of my neck, his mouth still at my ear. "What happened to my confident little nymph? Do you want to kneel for me or not?"

My insides melted at the prospect, my heart skipping a beat. "Yes," I said, louder, a needy moan slipping through at the end. No one but him could have heard it, but it gave me away completely. And the look darkening his expression confirmed it as he shifted back to study me.

"Now I want ninety minutes."

I swallowed. "Okay." I'd give him three hours if he wanted it.

He smiled. "Give me your wrist, Kailiani."

"Yes, sir," I whispered, holding up my hand.

"Oh, darling vixen, the things I am going to do to you…"

I quivered at the darkness of his words, suddenly wondering if I'd just made the biggest mistake of my life. But as his fingers wrapped around mine, I realized I had no choice.

Those were the rules.

Once an arrangement was struck, I could no longer negotiate.

And I'd just given him complete control with a few meager words of acceptance.

He pressed his watch to my cuff, his lips forming a predatory grin. "You're mine now, little siren."

Nero

Chapter Two

This was not part of the plan.

Alas, Kailiani wanted to play. So, we'd play.

However, I didn't believe this innocent act for a second.

No, she had something nefarious planned, just like the day she'd escaped me. And I couldn't wait to beat her at her own game.

Because I would not lose again.

Even if it meant fucking the truth out of her, something I'd enjoy since her body and heart were both owed to me. A deal struck generations ago, destroyed by her defiance.

Well, I had her now. And punishment would be served.

"I can think of worse punishments than having to kneel for you."

Mmm, that sassy little comment had hardened my cock

instantly. Fuck, just being near her again aroused me more than anyone or anything else had in the last millennium of my existence.

Which, of course, only made me hate her more.

That didn't mean I wouldn't take her first. It was my due, after all, and the dilation of her pupils said she wanted it, too.

Damn.

This was not how I'd anticipated our first reunion to go after all this time. I'd expected her to run, had even looked forward to the chase. Yet, she'd quite literally fallen at my feet, or had readily volunteered to.

Now it was time to see if she'd meant it.

With my palm against her exposed lower back, I guided her toward the two humans guarding the hallway of bedrooms. This whole new era of technology on Earth pleased me because it meant I didn't have to degrade myself by speaking to these unworthy creatures. I merely held out my watch, one of them scanned it, and the other escorted us to a room.

Brilliant.

Kailiani shivered as the door closed behind me, her big brown eyes sliding to the ground in a beautiful display of submission. How far would she take the act? Would she go as far as to allow me to fuck her? Or would she break before I had the chance?

The notion of it fluttered over my skin, exciting my nerves.

Oh, I wanted to test these boundaries, find out how far I could push before she caved.

"Remove the dress," I said, not bothering to waste any time. We only had ninety minutes, and I required all of them to win this little battle of wills.

Uncertainty lined her shoulders, confusing me. As a

siren, nudity shouldn't bother her in the slightest. She spent most of her life naked in the waves. Although, oddly, I couldn't scent the ocean on her.

When was the last time you went for a swim? I wanted to ask. Most of her kind couldn't stand to be on land for too long. They craved the sea, much as I did.

"Is there a problem?" I demanded.

"N-no. I'm just… Never mind." The tinge of fear in her tone confused me even more.

I almost fell for the act, almost asked her to finish the original sentence, but her spine straightened as if she'd made some sort of decision.

She lifted her nimble fingers to the straps of her dress to drag them over her shoulders to her lightly toned arms and then downward to expose her beautiful breasts. I'd seen them once upon a time, in the waves of our home. But I'd never been given the opportunity to touch them.

That would change tonight.

I would possess every inch of her. Every moan. Every breath. She wouldn't inhale without smelling the sea and my underlying power. And once she was addicted, I'd shatter her. Leave her to the depths of the ocean in despair, where she belonged.

No one defied me and got away with it.

Not even someone as gorgeous and alluring as my Kailiani.

But she deserved a special brand of discipline. One that would leave her alive and miserable and forever thinking of me.

The gown pooled at her feet, leaving her clad in a simple black thong.

Exquisite.

Her eyes remained downcast, the dark waves of her hair cascading over her shoulders like a black waterfall. So stunning. I couldn't wait to wrap those strands around my fist as I drove into her mouth.

Hmm, but first, I wanted to taste the forbidden fruit of my existence. The one who had escaped my grasp without a backward glance. The female who had nearly destroyed my soul by shattering our tentative bonds.

I grabbed the back of her nape—not so tenderly—and yanked her to me. Her lips parted on a gasp as I took her mouth in a vengeful kiss underlined in fury. A mortal would break beneath the pressure of my tongue, but Kailiani accepted it, her svelte siren form capable of withstanding wrath better than most.

Still, she trembled, flinching as I dominated her in a way only a god could.

If she'd hoped I would go easy on her, she'd thought wrong. I'd craved this moment for centuries, searching for her tirelessly. She was my single regret, the literal bane of my existence. My runaway betrothed, the one who'd disappeared on what should have been the most important day of our lives.

So, instead, I would have her on Earth. Tonight.

Not the ritual I had planned.

But it was the one she now deserved.

This would be degrading.

Painful.

And righteous.

She inhaled sharply as I finally released her, her eyes smoldering with arousal, not horror. Such a good little actress, pretending to like this. But I knew the truth, and she would soon admit it out loud.

I grabbed the elastic of her thong, snapping it with a flick of my wrist and sending the fabric to the floor with what appeared to be a key. Eyeing the item, I cocked a brow at her.

"For my apartment," she explained, her voice a breathy come-hither sound that made my balls ache.

And here I'd thought only blood could entertain me.

No, I wanted her wet in an entirely different way, and her bare mound would provide me with an unhindered view. "Go lie on the bed, knees up, legs spread. I want to see your cunt, Kailiani. Show me how much you want me."

Something we both knew she couldn't actually do, even if she wanted to fake it.

The body gave a woman away, and the second she showed me that dry pussy of hers, I'd have her right where I wanted her.

Her little pink tongue peeked at me as she wet her lower lip, her heart rate singing an escalated tune to my sensitive ears. *That's right, darling siren. You're trapped now.*

She swallowed and moved deeper into the reasonably sized bedroom. More windows overlooking the heavily polluted human city blinked back at us, their lights blinding and obnoxious compared to my sea realm. But they didn't seem to bother Kailiani. Her arms shook as she climbed up onto the four-poster bed, her trembles causing my lips to curl in triumph.

Until she lay on her back and did exactly as I'd told her to.

This was why I'd selected her all those years ago to be my queen.

She played me at every turn, always doing what I least expected.

Such as spreading her legs to give me a glorious view of her inviting center.

I loosened my tie as I stepped forward, her seductive heat beckoning me forward. Tossing my jacket to the side chair, I removed my cuff links and rolled the suffocating fabric of my dress shirt to my elbows. Then knelt on the mattress between her splayed thighs.

Fuck…

She wasn't just wet; she was drenched.

How is this possible?

Sirens were alluring by nature, but they couldn't force mutual attraction.

Which could only mean one thing—Kailiani wanted this. Was it our old bond she sensed? The power rippling through my veins? The idea of hurting me again?

I didn't know.

But I had to taste her.

Her gaze flickered down to mine as I bent my head between her shapely legs to lick her slick folds. She clutched the comforter on either side of her hips, a luscious moan sliding from her lips.

"Siren," I accused, sliding my tongue along her wet seam again. "You all make the sweetest little noises when you come. Shall I make you sing for me, Kailiani? Tantalize me with your screams?"

Her hips bucked in response, her rosy nipples turning rock hard above. It was a clear invitation to take this further, one I happily accepted with my mouth against her clit. She practically vibrated beneath my lips, her needy little bud pulsing and begging for the release only I could give her.

Oh, it was tempting to bring her to the precipice and engage in a game of denial. But I wanted to see what she would do, how she looked, how she *sounded* when she gave in to oblivion.

I slid a finger inside her, growling when I found her tight and soaked. Fuck, my dick would barely fit, but it would feel so damn good.

Where I belong…

No, I needed to see her climax first. Then she could

orgasm again around my shaft, while I made her regret ever turning her back on me.

Her thighs quivered around me, her inner walls clamping down around my finger. I'd barely begun my assault and already she was falling apart.

"Nero," she whispered, her back bowing off the bed on a wave of pleasure that had my balls throbbing. Her moans were soft, sweet, and far too quiet for my liking.

How strange. That wasn't very siren-like at all.

If I couldn't sense the water spirit residing within her, I'd almost call her human. Alas, I knew better. This was all part of her ploy.

I just needed to up my game.

"Next time, you don't come until I give you permission." I nipped her clit in reprimand, earning me a beautiful shriek in response.

There. *That* was more accurate.

She shuddered as I went to my knees, her luscious body shimmering with sweat. The droplets called to my powers, urging me to indulge my darker side, to truly make her pay. Sirens required water to thrive. If I removed the majority from her system, she'd wither and suffocate, but not necessarily die.

Oh, I could kill her. Immortality only meant she lived forever if a stronger being didn't destroy her. And I was by far her superior.

"I want you on your hands and knees," I told her, my voice a low growl. Part of me wanted to rip her apart, but the more sensual side desired to take what she offered, to finally claim my bride.

There were no vows here.

No future for us.

Only the now.

But I would revel in the beauty of owning her body and

soul, the memory one I knew would entertain me for centuries to come.

The day I finally won in this dangerous dance between us, for she was the only siren I'd ever desired. I still did, a fact that grated my nerves, but I'd just have to fuck it out of my system for good.

"Now," I commanded when she didn't immediately move.

She scurried upward, balancing on her hands and knees, her dark hair a curtain around her face. That wouldn't do at all. I wanted to see her eyes when I took her.

Standing, I removed my shirt, thankful to be rid of the claustrophobic fabric. My shoes, socks, and pants were next. No undergarments. Why humans fancied them, I'd never understand.

Crawling back up onto the bed, I positioned myself behind her and traced the curve of her spine with my index finger.

"Do you regret it, Kailiani?" I wondered. "What you've done?"

She shivered beneath my touch, her thighs visibly flexing. "N-no," she whispered.

"Mmm," I murmured, not surprised at all by her response. "I didn't think so." Which made this all the easier to do. I gathered her lush hair into my fist, fastening a makeshift harness.

She yelped as I tugged her head back, exposing her neck.

I leaned down to nip her thundering pulse. "You may change your mind, little siren."

Her responding whimper made me smile.

"Are you still wet for me?" I asked, reaching around to cup her breast—a perfect fit for my palm.

Because she was made for me.

That thought stoked the anger simmering through my veins, tightening my grip on her silky strands.

"Yes," she groaned. "Very wet."

Her words surprised me. My palm glided away from her chest to her abdomen and lower.

And shit, she was right.

"You're soaked," I marveled, gliding a finger through her core and sliding it inside her. She clenched around me, her needy little sex practically begging me to fuck her. "You want this."

"I do," she admitted, her voice a throaty purr that lit my blood on fire.

Impossible.

But the evidence of the truth saturated my finger.

Whatever it was that had her aroused, I didn't care. I wanted her with a ferocity I couldn't deny. It was as if her deception had heightened my desire for her. A weakness I needed to kill. Soon. However, not yet.

Tonight, I would indulge it.

I would indulge her.

"This won't be slow or painless," I warned her. Why I bothered was beyond me. Maybe because I yearned for her to fear me. Except all she did was tremble and press her ass up higher as if inviting me to enter her.

Topping from the bottom.

I'd allow it.

Only because I longed for the same outcome.

I slid my finger out of her and lifted it to her mouth. "Suck. Taste how badly you want me, Kailiani."

She parted her beautiful lips and took me deep, her little tongue stroking over my skin and giving me a brilliant idea of what it would be like to fuck her mouth.

One night won't be enough.

Good thing I had time to spare.

She swirled her tongue around the tip as I withdrew.

"So obedient," I praised, pleasantly surprised. "What do you want, Kailiani? Do you want me to fuck you?"

"Yes." It came out soft. Too soft.

"Tell me to fuck you, little siren." I pressed my length against her backside so she could feel my need for her. "Beg me for it."

She pressed into me, her neck arching beautifully as she looked over her shoulder at me. "Fuck me, Nero. *Please.*"

The words went straight to my gut, but it was her eyes that did me in. Two pools of dark chocolate imploring me to finish this—to *own* her.

I knew it was the siren calling to me.

Could feel her natural gift stroking my innate control over water.

But I ignored the knowledge and followed my instincts.

I wrapped my hand around the base of my cock and lined it up with her entrance. "Last chance, darling girl."

She wiggled enticingly, her gaze heated. "Fuck me," she repeated, the desire coating that command snapping my resolve.

I slammed into her with the force of the waves behind me, claiming her in the way she was meant to be claimed all those moons ago. And she screamed in response, her little body shaking beneath mine.

Not in a pleasurable way, but one filled with agony.

It was the sound I'd yearned for from her lips for so, so long, the same tormented cry that had left my own mouth the night she'd disappeared. Yet, rather than celebrate in her misery, I felt a tinge of remorse.

And so I stilled above her.

Waiting.

She hadn't fallen to the bed, her knees and hands still keeping her upright, but her head had lowered despite my

27

grasp on her hair. I wrapped my other arm around her middle, holding her as she shook violently.

Yes, I'd entered her hard. But she should have been able to handle it. She was fucking created to handle it.

"Talk to me, Kailiani," I said, hating the sound of concern in my voice. Why did I suddenly care? I wanted to destroy her. Not comfort her.

This is all probably a trick... Another fucking game.

"I'm okay." She didn't sound *okay.* "Just... shocked me."

Shocked her? How is—

She shifted, her walls clenching around me in a hypnotic way that drew a groan from my throat. "Fuck..." That felt too good. If she did that again, I wouldn't be able to just sit here. I'd have to finish it. I'd have to—

Another movement, this one purposeful, her backside brushing my groin with the temptation of her hips.

"Kailiani," I warned.

"Take me," she whispered. "Oh, God, I need you to move."

God, I thought, smiling. Her armor was cracking. She'd just addressed me by name.

"All right, little siren." Now we were back on the right sides of the court. *My* court. I slid out of her and thrust back in—hard—and she cried out in passion this time, not pain.

"Again," she begged, almost shocking me.

But I saw through her now.

Her siren call no longer applied.

I was in charge now.

And I demonstrated that by dominating her in the fiercest way I knew how, by driving into her little body with the force of all my power. I lowered myself over her back and used my fist in her hair to force her head to the side so I could take her mouth. The angle wasn't the best for her, but this was no longer about her pleasure. It was about mine.

I kissed her with the same harshness that I took her body, my tongue an impenetrable force against her own. She mewled against me, whether in protest or ecstasy, I couldn't tell. It all blended together as the god within me captured the reins.

Her pussy clamped down around me, hugging me with addictive little spasms that indicated her pending release. But she never let go, her body a tight bow of energy beneath me, waiting to be unleashed.

Because I'd told her not to come again without my permission.

How was it possible for her to be so fucking perfect? While also being the bane of my existence?

"Fuck, Kailiani..." I never expected this attraction or for it to feel so damn right between us. "I need you to come," I realized out loud, unable to keep the words to myself. "Come for me, darling vixen."

And she did.

She came apart on a moan directly into my mouth, my name a prayer from her tongue that sent me cascading over the falls into oblivion with her.

I erupted inside her, the force of it flooring me and causing me to see stars.

It'd *never* been like this, so intense, so overwhelming, so mindless. Violent quakes rocked around us, through us, binding our souls in a way they shouldn't.

And fulfilling the vows in a way that wasn't supposed to be possible.

Not on Earth.

Not with her.

How?

I collapsed beside her, my cock still fully erect and ready for another round while my mind rebelled.

Kailiani shook, still on her hands and knees, obeying me to the very end.

"Relax," I demanded, and she practically fell face-first into the mattress.

That was when I sensed the tears, my affinity for water calling on me to absorb them.

But that wasn't all I noticed.

Blood.

She'd bled on my dick.

My brow furrowed. What did that even mean? And why the hell was it red? Siren blood was blue.

I wrapped my palm around the back of her neck to force her to face me, and what I saw in her eyes tore a hole right through my soul.

Pain.

Distress.

Fear.

The very expression that I'd hoped to find the second she saw me tonight, but now found myself hating.

"Have I hurt you?" I heard myself asking, confused out of my mind.

She swallowed and started to shake her head, then nodded, and then shook her head again. "It's... not you."

"What is it?" I asked.

She tried to turn away, but I held her in place. "I just... I never expected... That is, I mean, I never anticipated my first time being... like that."

First time? Impossible. Kailiani wasn't a virgin. Sirens couldn't survive without sex.

"And now I'm embarrassed," she continued, attempting to hide again.

"Stop trying to look away," I commanded, needing to see her expression, her eyes, her *soul.*

Something wasn't right.

I sensed her—my Kailiani. She bore the same name and traits as my betrothed. But… "You bled on me."

"Oh, God…" Her cheeks turned bright red, the look on her actually quite adorable—and completely irrelevant. Because she'd just addressed me by name again.

"You know who I am," I said. Not a question, but a statement.

"Yes. Nero."

"My *real* name, Kailiani."

Wrinkles appeared on her forehead. "You told me your name is Nero. I… I don't know you by another name."

Had she meant the deity on Earth? One born of religious texts? Times had changed in the Human Realm since my last visit. I was no longer the one worshipped and feared, merely joked about in entertainment venues.

What if… what if this isn't a charade? I wondered, watching her closely for any hint of betrayal.

No sign of treachery.

Of course, I'd not noticed one all those years ago, either. But now I knew to look, and still, I saw nothing.

Had something happened to disrupt her memories? To put her soul in what appeared to be a human body?

But she'd not broken from the force of my thrusts.

So, what are you, my darling Kailiani?

My wrist buzzed with a warning of our ending session, causing me to wonder where the time had escaped to.

The vows, I realized. The force of our bonding—the *mating*—had surpassed time and space. Impossibly so, but I'd felt it.

We were connected now in the most intimate of ways. An act that should not have been possible.

I needed to confer with some of the others to determine what the fuck had just occurred. And more importantly, to figure out why Kailiani appeared to be human without any memory of the past.

"I'll be in touch," I said, releasing her. "Don't commit to anyone else." I'd feel it if she did, and a mortal male did not want to be on the receiving end of my possessive rage.

She remained silent while I washed up and dressed, her naked body lying splendidly across the mattress. It urged me to return to her, to take her all over again, but I couldn't. Not until I understood what in Hades's name was going on here.

But I did lean over to kiss her soundly once more, needing to brand her mouth with mine. "I mean it, Kailiani. No other commitments. I don't share." I nipped her lower lip hard enough to mark her, then laved the wound with my tongue, tasting her distinctly human blood. "See you soon, darling siren."

LIANI

CHAPTER THREE

CORBAN SAT BEHIND HIS BIG, oak desk, green eyes glimmering. "What did you do, Liani? Rob a bank?"

"No." I refused to tell him how I'd acquired the money, mostly because I still couldn't believe it myself.

Three days, and I still felt Nero between my thighs.

Not least of all because he'd taken me without protection —a fact that had me terrified. JBI had required a medical screening during my interview, and implanted an IUD as well, but that wouldn't protect me from contracting something from a client who refused to use a condom.

"Liani," Corban snapped, pulling my focus back to him. My gaze had drifted out the window, to the Hudson beyond.

"Yes?"

"Tell me where the money came from."

I cleared my throat and sat up a little straighter. "Why does it matter? You have what you need—a down payment in good faith. I'll continue working until I earn the rest." *Assuming JBI contacts me.* It'd been several days since my audition and no word from JBI or Mister "I don't share." Not that I really expected to hear from either. They'd confiscated my cuff and sent me home directly after I exited the bedroom, stating I was too disheveled to continue working.

Which meant I was short the one grand I should have earned at the end of the night.

But Nero's ninety-minute session payment made up for the difference, and then some.

Corban rubbed the blond scruff dotting his square jaw, his pupils little pinpoints of displeasure. "Your mother kept secrets from me. Look where that got you."

I bristled at the mention of the reason I'd landed in this mess. "Well, unlike her, I won't be running."

"No, you won't," he agreed. "Because I'll find you, Liani. And you won't like what happens when I do."

"You asked for a show of good faith, and you have one. I'll get the rest of your money; I just need time."

"Now you sound just like her."

"Well, I'm not her," I fired back, insulted by the relation. "She never paid you back a dime." *And she threw her own daughter under the bus.* Something I would never do to anyone, least of all my child.

But I hadn't been raised in a fairy tale. No, quite the opposite. I learned from a very young age how to fend for myself. It was what had prompted me to excel in school, to achieve all the best grades and earn a full-ride scholarship to NYU.

Too bad my mother had destroyed my senior year with

all this bullshit. I'd been a semester shy of graduating when her life had imploded in my face.

The day she'd introduced me to Corban.

An internship, she'd called it.

Yeah, some internship that turned out to be.

He relaxed his broad shoulders on a shrug. "All right. Bring me a similar payment in ten days, and I'll give you more slack."

"Ten days?" I squeaked.

"Go rob another bank, or whatever it is you did." The devilish glint in his irises said he knew exactly what I'd done. Which wouldn't surprise me. His men had been following me for weeks to make sure I didn't run. "It'll bring you to about ten percent of what your mother owes me. Some would call that generous on my part, to even contemplate a down payment. Especially considering your mother's track record."

I gritted my teeth and swallowed a complaint. Because none would matter. If I didn't produce the funds as he required, he'd find a different way for me to earn him money. One not too dissimilar to that of the other night, except then it would be on his terms and not mine.

If only this had happened six months *after* my college graduation and not before. Then maybe I would have found a day job.

Alas, no one wanted to hire someone with a mostly completed business degree.

"I'll have it to you in ten days," I said, mustering a confidence I didn't feel.

How I would manage it was another issue entirely. But I lacked a choice in the matter. I either figured it out or paid the price of my mother's sins.

"I like you, Liani," he said softly. "Let's keep it that way."

A subtle threat, one that scattered goose bumps along my sweater-clad arms. *How my mother ever trusted this man...* I fought the urge to shake my head and stood instead. "See you soon, Corban."

"Yes. You will." He dismissed me with a wave of his elegant hand, his gold ring glistening in the late afternoon sun streaming in through his office windows.

His bodyguard stood waiting at the door, the ugly white scar adorning his cheek and jaw seeming to mock me. He didn't smile. He didn't speak. He merely twisted the handle and escorted me down the pristine hallway and deposited me in the elevator without so much as a glance.

I collapsed against the steel walls, alone at last, and let out the shaky breath I'd been holding. "What are you doing?" I whispered to myself, cringing.

If JBI didn't hire me, I was fucked.

When I asked Veronica about it this morning, she said JBI would be in touch either way, and at this point, no news was actually good news. Because it meant they were likely going through the process of bringing me on.

"It's much easier to dismiss someone," she'd said.

I hope you're right, I thought for the thousandth time.

But I couldn't rely on her, or JBI, or anyone other than myself. That was the one lesson my mother had instilled in me in life.

The doors opened into an expansive lobby lined with marble and gold, and two more of Corban's goons. They watched as I made my way across the floor, my heels clacking with every step.

Then I was outside.

Free.

For now.

"Name three adjectives that describe you," the restaurant manager said, his attention on the notepad in his sweaty palms. He'd barely been able to meet my gaze when I'd arrived, making me question his managerial position.

"Punctual, efficient, and kind," I replied, using the politest voice I could muster.

He nodded, writing that down.

"Tell me about a time when you faced a difficult customer situation"—he squinted at the scribbles on his pad —"and how you resolved it."

This had to be the worst interview ever. At least my audition for JBI had been interesting.

And, well, pleasing.

I gave him an example, then answered some of his other canned questions before shaking his too-damp hand and leaving the pizzeria.

Interview number five—done.

I had two more this week, and less than seven days to come up with the funds for Corban. Despair hung just over my head, threatening to pour all over my future. But I extended my metaphorical umbrella to keep the storm clouds at bay and forced myself to walk the six blocks back to my studio apartment.

There was still time.

I could do this.

I had to.

There was no other—

A package on my doorstep had me pausing in the hallway, my brow furrowing. The label was addressed to me, but I hadn't ordered anything.

I unlocked the door, picked it up, and entered my tiny studio. After bolting the lock behind me, I turned my focus to the box.

No return address.

Handwritten.

"Odd." I carefully unwrapped it and gasped at the dark blood-red dress lying inside. Elegant handwriting adorned the card sitting on top of the fabric.

For tonight.

—N

I read it twice, not understanding. Then went in search of my phone—I'd left it charging while at my interview. Not exactly the safest plan, but the battery was almost dead and I didn't have to walk too far to the restaurant.

A voicemail and two text messages sat waiting for me.

All from JBI.

"Hello, Miss Mikos. Your audition was a success. A new phone will be delivered to you via courier in precisely two hours. However, you already have an interested client. As we have no other means of contacting you, a current client offer will be sent through text message. Should you have any questions upon review, please give our offices a call. Welcome to JBI, Miss Mikos. We look forward to our profitable journey together."

I blinked, stunned.

Then read the first message.

One-week assignment. No packing required. Dress and shoes will be provided for tonight's dinner.

"Uh, okay." That didn't tell me anything. Like where I would be staying, what he wanted from me, or even a name. Although, the card with the package indicated it was Nero. Still, a little more detail would be appreciated.

The second text said: *Pickup scheduled for six.*

So, I didn't even get to agree to the terms? No contractual review? Just an expectation that I accepted?

Which, yeah, I wasn't really in a position to deny anything at the moment. Nor did I really want to...

Nero had been passionate. Hot. Demanding. And so

fucking sexy. My lady parts tingled at the thought of another night with him. A completely insane reaction after the rough way he'd handled me, but there'd been a hint of tenderness, too.

And possessiveness.

I shivered at the thought. He'd commanded me with every touch, then sealed his ownership with a gaze before he left.

"Don't commit to anyone else." His words had branded my mind, making it impossible for me to even consider engaging in an arrangement with another man. A ludicrous reaction when I hardly knew him.

Oh, but I gave my virginity to him.

Willingly.

Mostly.

And also for money.

Which made me a whore for hire.

Awesome.

I clenched my teeth and swallowed a growl. Belittling myself wasn't the answer. Accepting, however, was, because I needed that money. Of course, I had no idea how much he was offering.

A week? Doing what? Living where? Here?

My lips pinched to the side. I had JBI's number saved in my phone, something they'd requested during the prolonged interview process. And I used it now.

Might as well see what they had in mind, and how best to prepare myself. Because there was no doubt in my mind that I would be accepting. I just wanted to know the details.

And also, maybe, to make sure it was Nero who had booked me.

He said he didn't share, and I believed him.

What is this madness? I wondered with a sigh, lifting the

phone to my ear. *Why do I feel compelled to bow to him? Better yet, why did I want to?*

The notion of kneeling at his feet sent a thrill down my spine, heating my blood. No one had ever evoked such a response from me, hence my former virginity. But Nero, he'd lit me on fire with a glance, as if awakening a part of me that lay dormant just waiting for his nearness and touch.

I closed my eyes, picturing his chiseled features and dark, ocean-blue eyes.

Please let this offer be from him.

A female answered on the third ring. "Hello, Liani," she greeted me. "Are you calling regarding your offer?"

"I am." I nibbled my lower lip, my eyes still closed, Nero a painting I refused to stop envisioning. "It said it was for a week, but the client's name wasn't included."

"Yes, to protect his privacy, of course. Text messages are so easily shared, particularly from a personal phone. That's why we're issuing you a company mobile—one that is controlled and monitored by JBI. Is now a good time to review the details of the client's request?"

"It is." I gripped my small kitchen table for support, suddenly needing it. "I would like to hear the entirety of the offer, including any requirements and where I will be staying for the next week."

"Of course. One moment while I pull up the contract on file from Mister Rotanev."

My eyes opened, my brow furrowing. *Mister Rotanev?*

"Ah, yes, here we are. He's requested a week in his Manhattan residence, no hard limits, and he says everything will be paid for, so no packing required. We also couriered over a dress for you this evening, at his request. Did you receive it?"

"I did, but what do you mean by 'no packing required'? It's a week-long stay."

"Mister Rotanev will be providing everything you need, including clothing, if he so wishes."

Meaning he might not allow me to wear anything at all. Thus, the no-limits requirement. "What is Mister Rotanev's first name?" I asked, a lump forming in my throat.

"Nero, Miss Mikos. But I recommend you address him as 'sir' or 'Mister Rotanev,' unless he states otherwise." A hint of censure entered her tone, as if she were a teacher scolding a student. Given the relief her words had provided, however, I didn't mind.

"Yes, of course. Thank you. I accept."

"No negotiation? And you don't require the financial details?" She sounded surprised. As she should since money was my primary reason for doing this.

What the hell is wrong with me? Accepting just because it's Nero? I shook my head. "I would like to hear his full offer."

"Keep in mind, you can always negotiate, and most of our employees do." With that, she gave me a figure that had my jaw dropping to the floor.

"For seven nights?" I squeaked.

"Yes, with no limits. As I said, counteroffers are expected. This is just the initial estimate."

My lips were moving without sound because I couldn't believe that was just the baseline. It more than covered the amount Corban wanted next week. Hell, it almost covered the total amount *owed*. "I-I…"

"Might I suggest a twenty percent increase as a counteroffer? I believe that to be a conservative play in this situation."

A twenty percent increase?! Holy shit. "Is that, uh, normal?"

"Yes." No elaboration, just a firm response.

"O-okay," I replied, my stomach in knots.

"I'll have it drafted and sent. Would a text message

confirmation be acceptable? Or would you prefer another call?"

"Uh, a text is fine."

"Excellent. May I assist you with anything else, Miss Mikos?"

Yeah, you can help me find my mind. Because I'm pretty sure I lost it somewhere five minutes ago. Instead of saying that out loud, I cleared my throat and voiced a negative, adding, "Thank you," to the end.

"Anytime, Miss Mikos. Welcome to JBI." She hung up, leaving me staring at my phone.

"Holy hell…" How was this happening? Seven nights with Nero for a tiny fortune. "*Shit.*"

A new text came through not even two minutes later.

It displayed two words that made my heart jump.

Counteroffer accepted.

NERO

CHAPTER FOUR

KAILIANI MIKOS WAS DEFINITELY HUMAN. The photographic proof of her adolescence provided a telling tale, as did several key background details.

She had a mortal mother.

Was definitely a virgin prior to our night together—something her JBI health report had helpfully proven.

Attended a university until recently.

Resided in a tiny closet of a space far less appealing than my palatial estate.

And she was seeking employment in dire establishments.

Somehow, some way, the treacherous female of my past had died, only to be resurrected as the bride I'd once coveted.

The question became: How did I call the siren inside of her to the surface? Because this human shell she wore was too fragile, and I refused to be held captive by the mistress of time.

Mortals died.

Gods did not.

I rejected the fate lurking before us, desiring my betrothed for eternity, as was my due.

Because this woman—the one walking toward me right now—could very well be a future goddess.

The red fabric swam over her curves, giving her a liquid appeal that called to my very soul. *Blood water.* That was what the gown resembled. Alluring, deadly, and oh-so sensual.

She'd gathered her dark hair up into a messy bun with ringlets hanging tantalizingly over her shoulders. I wanted to fondle them, to test their soft texture, and kiss her plump, rose-tinted lips until she couldn't breathe.

Alas, I held myself steady, choosing to admire her instead as she wove through the crowd near the entrance.

JBI wouldn't allow me to retrieve her myself, proclaiming it to be a security condition. Ridiculous, considering anyone who could afford their services could easily afford to purchase a detailed background report as well—which would include addresses. But I played their little game, choosing to maintain this absurd billionaire facade. They saw me as powerful because of my bank account and stature.

Oh, how those mortals had no idea what power truly entailed.

I could bring this entire room to their knees in a second. Dominate the city in a single breath.

My lips curled at the thought. One wave and all the pretty little humans would perish. Including the one now standing before me.

No, that wouldn't do. I rather liked this version of my female. Apart from the breakable aspect, anyway.

"Hello, Kailiani," I murmured, wrapping my palm around the back of her neck and declaring to all the pitiful beings in the room that this gorgeous creature belonged to me.

"Good evening, Mister Rotanev." Sensuality swirled in her voice, the siren within her begging to come out to play.

Soon, my darling pet. We'll find a way to free you.

That was why I'd booked her for a week. Although, the cheeky little minx sent me a counteroffer. I didn't mind paying more—money was a human commodity that translated to nothing in my world. However, the defiance of her act, well, that required punishment.

Mmm, but not until I kissed her. I needed a taste before we truly engaged in this seductive dance between us.

"Call me Nero," I whispered, pulling her into me. "Or 'sir,' if you prefer." I brushed my mouth over hers, loving the way her lips parted in response. Such a natural seductress despite her obvious innocence.

I accepted her unspoken invitation and slid my tongue into her mouth, my grip tightening against her neck. Her delicate hands curled around my jacket, holding on while I devoured her the way I craved.

Energy hummed around us, my power rippling through the air and encasing us in an impenetrable shell, protecting my chosen mate on instinct alone.

She was meant to be mine all those years ago.

Had nearly destroyed me with her escape.

But now I had her again, and this time, she had nowhere to go.

Kailiani would kneel before me tonight and worship me as a siren should worship her god. Because I willed it. Because I'd earned it. Because I desired it.

She gasped as I released her, gulping in oxygen, her cheeks inflamed in a delicious shade of lust. A state I intended to escalate throughout our evening together.

"Come, Kailiani. I have a reservation for us." I pressed my palm to her exposed lower back. The front of her dress displayed only a teasing amount of cleavage, but this gown was all about the subtle reveals—the slits up both her thighs and the back that nearly exposed the top of her ass.

And she wore it beautifully.

My goddess.

The host led us to our table—a corner booth that gave us a view of the entire restaurant while affording a semblance of privacy. I'd chosen it with a purpose in mind, something Kailiani would be learning soon.

"Here we are," the host announced, gesturing to the U-shaped booth. It was large enough to seat six, which caused Kailiani to frown as she tried to figure out where to sit. She chose the edge while I slid in from the other side toward the middle.

"Come sit beside me," I told her, amused by her nervous tells. Sirens were confident in nature, the type to take charge, especially with men. But this one had been raised by humans, which had clearly encouraged her submissive nature. A seductive combination.

The host left us with a pair of menus that I ignored in favor of the beauty beside me. "You don't need to fear me, Kailiani." Most did, and should, but not her.

And how ironic was that? A week ago, I'd intended to flay her alive before feeding her to the deepest bowels of the ocean.

Now, I would give anything to protect her—*my mate.*

Oh, if this all turned out to be some sort of nefarious act, I'd kill her. But there was no denying her mortal shell. Something sinister was at play here. I could taste it in the air surrounding her. Yet, she seemed completely oblivious to it.

Her mutual attraction was real, as was her unmistakable acquiescence.

What happened to you, my darling siren?

"I'm not afraid," she finally said, her words measured and smooth. "I just... Well, I barely know you."

Hmm, true. While I knew almost every detail about her, my background and name would mean very little to her.

Oh, she surely knew all about the Poseidon of mythology. But that wasn't me at all, just the human interpretation of my existence. One I found quite humorous, as did the other gods who were immortalized during that era.

Mortals sure loved their stories.

I stretched my arm out across the back of the booth, just above her slender shoulders, and angled my body toward her. "All right. Ask me anything you want."

The widening of her gaze suggested she hadn't expected me to say that at all. Which, considering what she'd just admitted to—not knowing me well—made sense.

"I'm an open book, Kailiani," I added softly, meaning it. Whatever she desired to know, I'd tell her. It just might be more of a riddle than an answer, but her mortal mind wasn't ready for the full truth of my presence here or what it meant for her. *That* would be explained as soon as I figured out how her siren soul had become trapped inside a human body.

She licked her lips, her eyes telegraphing her thoughts. She didn't want to dig too deep for risk of angering me, but she plainly possessed a multitude of questions.

I waited patiently, my thumb teasing the strap of her dress. It would be so easy to knock it from her shoulder and expose her breast to my gaze. Of course, the rest of the room would see her as well, and that would not do.

No, this woman was mine.

And I did not share.

"What, uh, do you do for a living?" she asked.

"Such a safe question," I teased, not at all surprised she'd chosen that route. "I hold a position of management." Specifically, the Aquaine Kingdom of the Mythios Realm. "There are a few million beings who thrive under my direction." Closer to five million, really. All the water creatures of Mythios existed under my command, as did the seas themselves. And I supposed, technically, while I lived on Earth, everything water-related here fell to my power, too.

Not that I'd exhibited any of my abilities. The last thing I wanted to do was piss off the supernatural beings managing the entry and exit points on Earth. Unfortunately, they had the political power to send me home. Which meant I had to play by their rules.

For now.

"You have over a million employees?" she whispered, her awe adorable.

"No, I only employ a handful beneath my direct command." Mainly my generals, like Maheer. "But yes, my management applies to several million."

"What do you manage? Like, what industry?"

"I suppose you could say I work for the oceans."

"As in, environmental health? Or something similar?"

"Exactly." I smiled. "I ensure water is clean, pure, and healthy." Which was why I hated this realm. They treated the oceans here as waste sites, not as something to be cared for and respected.

"Interesting. Did you study oceanography?"

I chuckled. "You could say that, I suppose." But I hadn't gone to school for it. Water was my natural ally, my primary mistress. "What about you, Kailiani? How do you feel about the oceans?"

She frowned. "Well, I've always loved to swim."

No surprise there.

"But I've not really had the opportunity to swim in the ocean," she continued. "I mean, it's all around New York City, but it's not something I've indulged in, I guess."

Interesting. Perhaps that would lead to unleashing her siren soul? Or maybe I needed to take her home? It would be easy to do, but the uncertainty of whether I could truly trust her held me back. Just an instinct that something wasn't quite right, despite her perceived innocence.

"Are you married?" she blurted out, causing me to snort.

Such a mortal question to ask. "No." Not by her definition, anyway. The Human Realm ritual married corporal bodies —a superficial union that existed only on the surface. Such a tenuous link and very unlike the connections formed in my world.

The souls of Mythios bonded for eternity. It was how I had recognized Kailiani beyond her physical appearance. My soul knew hers because we'd exchanged promises once upon a time.

Promises that had blossomed into a vow the other night, marking us as mates in the oldest of ways.

Which, I supposed, did mean I was married.

To her.

Until death do us part.

I smiled. Definitely not something to explain just yet. "Go on, my little siren. What else do you really want to know? Beyond these frivolous queries. Ask me something more pressing."

She swallowed, her gaze falling to my mouth before lifting to refocus on my eyes. "What do you have planned for me?"

Ah, there we were, the true cause for her nerves. "Everything," I promised. "You're mine, Kailiani."

"For a week, yes."

Oh, no, darling siren. For far longer than that. But her comment reminded me of the task I had in mind for her. "Yes, only seven days. Which means we should get right to the point. I'd love to know what that twenty percent counter acceptance earns me. Perhaps you could demonstrate for me now. Preferably with your pretty little mouth."

I didn't really care so much about the price as I did about her boldness in negotiating with me. I wanted to test that courage, see how far it went.

"That... I mean, I wasn't, uh..." She trailed off, her gaze dropping to my lips again. "With my mouth?"

The waiter chose that moment to interrupt, something that would have earned him severe punishment in my world. Alas, humans were governed beneath a different set of societal rules.

"Just water for now," I said before he could speak. "I'll signal you when we're ready for more."

"Right, yes, sir." He bowed a little, then straightened with a frown and wandered off.

I dismissed him immediately, my attention solely on the gorgeous being beside me. "Yes, with your mouth."

"H-how?" she breathed, the single word music to my ears.

I glanced around the restaurant, noting how everyone was engrossed in their meals and conversations. "I doubt anyone will notice you slipping to your knees beneath our table, darling. Particularly considering the skirt skims the ground and hides everything from view." I returned my eyes to her now widening ones. "Don't you agree?"

"You want me to... *here?*"

"Consider it an appetizer," I murmured just as our waiter returned.

Kailiani didn't acknowledge him or the glasses he set on

the table, too busy gaping at me. I ignored him as well, hoping to send a clear message.

Fortunately, he received it.

"What if someone sees me?" she asked after he walked away again.

"I sort of hope they do," I admitted. "But you'll be too busy under the table to notice or care about them anyway."

"I... I..."

I cocked a brow. "You didn't kneel for me the other night yet had the nerve to charge me an increased sum for our week together. I'd almost say it's my due, wouldn't you?" I meant it as a taunt, hoping to provoke the confident woman within.

The flare of her pupils said I'd hit the mark, while the flush creeping up her cheeks suggested my request aroused her.

And that alone had my cock hardening behind the zipper of my slacks.

"Unless that's too daring for you," I goaded her, tilting my head to the side, waiting for her confirmation. I saw the approval simmering in the dark depths of her gaze, could scent her sensual interest on the air.

Yet, she said nothing. A taunt in and of itself.

Then she looked around and slid to her knees beneath the table.

Oh, this would be wicked fun indeed.

LIANI

CHAPTER FIVE

I can't believe I'm doing this, I thought as my knees hit the hard floor. My thighs clenched in anticipation, my mouth watering for a taste of Nero in his sexy-as-sin suit.

Something was seriously wrong with me. I shouldn't be turned on by this, or enjoying his dark proclivities, but from the moment he told me his desire, it'd become mine as well. And now I'd be damned if I tried to stop myself.

What was more, I wanted to prove my worth to him. To seduce and please him so thoroughly that he didn't doubt once why he'd chosen me.

I wanted to make him beg for more.

He spread his legs to accommodate me as I settled between his knees, my palms on his upper thighs. Everything in his posture screamed nonchalance, as if he wasn't at all intrigued by my presence at his feet.

That was about to change.

I slid my hand upward to his belt, deftly undoing the buckle. Heat emanated from his groin, taunting my fingers as I unbuttoned his dress pants and drew down his zipper.

No boxers or briefs.

Just pure man.

And damn, that was hot.

I gripped his thick shaft, eager to touch him and explore. The other night hadn't afforded me the opportunity to get up close and personal with him. Not like this. And now I craved the ability to truly feel him.

So soft.

I shifted forward, thankful for the higher table, and bent to lick the pre-cum from his head. A groan caught in my throat at the salty, masculine flavor. This was an act I'd never imagined myself wanting to do, but with Nero, I absolutely wanted to proceed. Not only that, but I also wanted to own him with my mouth, to put all of his previous experiences to shame.

A tall order for someone like me—someone lacking in training and exposure to such acts—but I didn't let it stop me. My instincts took over, driving my mouth down over his cock and taking him as deep as my throat allowed.

He palmed the back of my head, holding me in place when I would have backed off to breathe, and pushed me an inch farther, testing my gag reflex.

I relaxed, trusting him, and focused on accepting his girth instead of reacting. Then the pressure eased, and he allowed me to rise just enough to inhale before guiding me back down again.

I grasped the base of his erection, giving it a squeeze as I fought to swallow enough of him to touch my lips to my skin.

His fingers knotted in my hair in response, pulling the strands tightly as his legs flexed around me.

Mmm, a sign of approval, I thought, pleased.

And repeated the action.

"Yes, we would," Nero said, his voice a deep rumble. It took me a moment to realize he was speaking to the waiter. He rattled off a bottle of wine and requested two glasses. The bored quality of his tone forced me to work harder, sucking him deeper and swirling my tongue over his head as I came up for air.

His muscles were solid on either side of me, his fingers a vise against my scalp, but he continued speaking to the waiter in the most nonchalant manner while ordering our dinners.

I skimmed my teeth across his sensitive flesh in silent reprimand, demanding a reaction from him. One I received in the form of a low growl that I felt all the way to my core. It was the kind of sound a woman wanted to hear while being fucked within an inch of her life.

Similar to the other night.

Desiring to hear it again, I continued my onslaught, applying more pressure and intensity with my mouth. And he rewarded me by flexing his hips upward, seeking more depth. If the waiter remained nearby, I didn't hear him. But he no longer mattered, only Nero and the orgasm I felt rising beneath my tongue.

I needed him to come so badly it almost hurt. Mostly because I had to taste him, to swallow him, to claim some small part of him in this intrinsically instinctual manner.

His touch shifted to my nape, holding me to him in a less demanding fashion. Because he wanted to give me an opportunity to move? Not a chance. I craved this more than air, and I demonstrated that by hollowing my cheeks, commanding him with my mouth to unleash everything he had down my waiting throat.

He squeezed my neck only once, providing an unspoken signal of his impending release just before he erupted with hot jets of cum across my expectant tongue. I swallowed him thoroughly, accepting every drop and moaning in response to how right it felt to receive him in this way.

Never before had I wanted to drink from a man, but with Nero, I wanted to bathe in his masculinity, luxuriate in his presence, and absorb every inch of him into my very soul.

It made no sense.

I'd just met him.

I barely knew him.

And yet, I felt as if I'd known him for several lifetimes.

What is happening to me?

I didn't do insta-love, or love in general. No, this wasn't that. Maybe insta-lust? Yes, that seemed more accurate. But what was this deep connection to him? Why did I yearn to submit to his every command?

Even now, I licked him clean, making sure I left him spotless before returning him to his trousers. Then waited between his legs before he gave me permission to rise.

It just felt so natural.

So real.

So *me*.

Like I'd been lost for years and only Nero had the ability to bring out the woman I longed to be.

Not necessarily the submissive, but an adventurous vixen.

A woman who sucked a man off in public without caring what anyone thought.

A woman who gave her virginity willingly during a night of heated passion with a stranger.

He released my neck and drew his thumb across my jaw to my lips. I kissed the thick pad and licked it as he dipped it inside my mouth.

"You're perfect," he rumbled from above. "Come here. I want to see your freshly fucked mouth, Kailiani."

I moved carefully upward, returning to my seat and looking directly at him instead of the rest of the room. Who cared if anyone saw me? One look at Nero and they'd have to understand why. The man was a fucking god among men.

He palmed my cheek and drew me to him for a kiss that seared my insides. I practically melted into him, my legs clenching at the intensity radiating from my core. A whimper slipped from my mouth to his, the need for him to touch me nearly undoing my ability to sit upright.

"I'm starting to think you enjoyed that more than I did," he murmured, licking my lower lip. "Mmm, one moment." He pulled away to address the waiter standing by our table with a bottle of wine. "Proceed."

Our poor waiter looked ready to faint as he held the bottle out for Nero's inspection, his nervousness at interrupting us evident in the way his hand shook. I almost pitied the guy, but the sight of a familiar face across the room had me forgetting all about him.

Veronica.

She gave me a knowing look, then cocked her head toward the left. I followed the gesture to the signs for the bathroom.

Didn't take a genius to figure out what she wanted.

"I approve." Nero's comment was in regard to the wine.

I leaned into him. "I'm going to go freshen up in the ladies' room."

His palm grasped my thigh before I could move, and he dipped his head to my ear. "Sure. Just remember, you're not allowed to come without my permission." He nipped my lobe, his words causing my insides to melt.

He thought I wanted to go *relieve* myself.

"That's not—"

"Go, Kailiani," he whispered. "Hurry back and remember what I said."

He squeezed my leg and released me, sending a fresh wave of heat over my already hot body.

Oh, God. This man...

I shook my head and forced myself to move. Otherwise, I'd probably end up under the table again.

Awareness trickled up my spine as I walked, Nero's gaze a brand against my back. There was no doubt in my mind who owned me in this moment. I would happily remain here, basking in his attentions forever. Not practical, but nothing about dreaming was ever considered realistic.

Veronica stood waiting for me just inside the bathroom while pretending to touch up her overdone eye makeup. She batted her lush, dark lashes at me and smiled. "I take it you got the job?"

Ah, right. In my hurry to prepare for Nero today, I'd forgotten to text her and give her a heads-up. Since she was the one who'd introduced me to JBI, and vouched for me, I definitely owed her a debt of gratitude. "Yes. They just called a few hours ago."

"And you already have a date?" She smiled, waggling her eyebrows. "A sexy one, too, from the looks of it."

"He's... yeah." I had no words to describe Nero Rotanev.

"I bet he's kinky as fuck." The statement was pitched low, for my ears alone. "I mean, there has to be a reason a man that good-looking needs, well, *us*." She giggled and started applying lipstick. "Of course, most of them are just too busy succeeding in life and want something noncommittal with an expected end date."

I frowned at her words, mostly because of the truth behind it. "Is it normal to spend a week with them?"

"Oh yeah. I've got mine through the weekend." She

grimaced, then shrugged. "But it's worth it."

"What's the longest you've done?"

"About a month, but Sophia just spent two years with hers." Veronica's hazel eyes met mine in the mirror. "Honestly, I think she had begun to believe it was love. But he dropped her for a fresh new thing just last week. Sophia's a complete wreck over it."

I didn't know Sophia, but I felt for her. Two years had to feel like a breakup. *What if Nero kept me on for that long?* He said he didn't share, made it very clear that he didn't want me to schedule anyone else. Would he do the same? Had he already done that to someone else at JBI? I knew nothing about his background, nothing about whom he had purchased before me.

"So let that be a lesson to us all," Veronica continued, oblivious to my thoughts. "Never get attached, because they certainly won't. You'll be discarded the second he finds his next pretty conquest."

Her comment, while meant to apply in general, stung. Because I had felt something forming between me and Nero that could be *more*. I couldn't explain it, just an instinct that had me feeling far too comfortable in his presence.

But she was right.

This arrangement could only be temporary.

Not only as a result of him hiring me to please him, but also because I had no intention of making this a long-term endeavor. Once I had the funds to pay off Corban, I was done. I'd finish school and leave New York City for good.

"Earth to Liani," Veronica said, waving a hand before my eyes. "You've totally spaced out on me."

"Sorry, I'm just exhausted."

She smirked. "All that work under the table?"

My cheeks heated in response. "I thought we weren't allowed to talk about any of this?" It was in the contract I had signed during the interview process. Client confidentiality was extremely important to JBI for obvious reasons.

"Yeah, yeah. As you're my childhood bestie, I think we're fine." She winked and picked up her purse. "But I should get back to my date before he wonders what's taking me so long. I just wanted to say hi!" She wrapped her arms around me and squeezed. "Welcome to my secret life."

I scoffed at that. "Not a secret when I already knew, V." She'd been involved with JBI since right after high school, and while she never shared the dirty details, I knew what she did for a living. It was the path she chose instead of college. Now that I saw the financial benefits, I understood why. She could always go to school later—and pay for it up front— when she tired of dating rich guys for cash.

"Yeah, yeah. But I only let you skim the surface. Now you'll be as deep as me and *really* get it." She pulled away with a wink. "Oh, and hey, at least he'll help you fix that V-card problem you've been carrying around."

"Veronica!" I smacked her arm, my face turning beet red in the reflection of the mirror.

"Oh my God. He already did, didn't he?!" She guffawed so loudly that the woman entering the bathroom actually paused to gape at her. Not that Veronica noticed. She often existed in her own world. "How was it?"

"You know I can't answer that," I hissed.

"Oh, come on. You can give me an enthusiastic smile that I can interpret appropriately, or continue scowling like that, which I don't believe for a second."

I just shook my head. "You're incorrigible."

"And you're totally holding out on me."

"You know why."

She sighed dramatically. "We need a tequila date. That'll help you talk."

"I hate tequila."

"No, dear. You hate what tequila does to you." She patted me on the head and smiled. "Now fix your hair. You look like you were just fucked in the face." She winked and pranced out of range before I could playfully hit her arm again.

"Go enjoy your night," I told her, then checked my appearance in the mirror.

And yeah, she was right. I'd been focused on my flushed cheeks before. Now I saw the mess on my head. Everyone in the restaurant probably thought I was going for a messy, just-got-out-of-bed look and was failing to pull it off.

"You, too." She blew a kiss at me. "Toodle-oo, ho."

I glared at her back. "Takes one to know one."

She flipped me off with a laugh and disappeared, leaving me to clean up. My dark strands were held up with an abundance of pins, most of which had shifted, thanks to Nero's fingers.

Note to self: Don't bother with an updo going forward. He'll just destroy it.

Also note to self: Stop planning for the future. Because there isn't one.

I gave myself a once-over while holding on to that thought for dear life and headed back to the table. Nero's oceanic gaze swam over me, his approval evident in the way he tilted one corner of his mouth. My lips refused to return the smile, mostly because I was too busy trying to ignore his charming spell.

Which failed immediately as he wrapped his arm around me and pulled me to his side. "What's wrong, darling siren? Are you sour with me for delaying your gratification?"

Oh, I'd completely forgotten about *that*. But now that he brought it up again, my hormones roared back to life with a vengeance, causing me to squirm beside him.

He pressed his lips to my temple and then to my ear. "Or was it the friend you just met in the bathroom?"

I stilled. "What?"

"I'm an observant man, Kailiani. I saw her gesture to you from across the restaurant, too." He kissed my pulse before pulling away to meet my gaze. "Who is she?"

"Uh, someone from my childhood." I swallowed, unsure of how much to say. "She's, well, she's the one who helped me get the job with…"

"JBI?" he finished for me. "Why did you choose to work for them?"

"Why did you choose to contract with them?" I countered, raising a brow.

His lips twitched. "If I give you my reason, will you give me yours?"

Not the reply I expected. "I… yes." I just wouldn't elaborate on it.

"I wanted you," he said, smiling. "That's why I agreed to be a client."

My brow furrowed. "What? You weren't already a client when I met you last weekend?"

He traced my lower lip with his thumb, his opposite arm tightening around my shoulders. "No, that was my first JBI experience. Definitely a memorable one, wouldn't you agree?"

"Y-yes." More than memorable, but that comment wasn't what captivated my attention. "You weren't a client before Friday?"

"I already answered that." He tapped me on the nose and settled beside me. "I rarely, if ever, frequent New York City. I prefer the Mediterranean region. That said, it's actually quite rare for me to be in your realm for extended periods in general, let alone in a highly populated area."

I wasn't sure how to interpret his statement, but my

mouth was moving without consulting my brain. "Is that why you need me? To help you pass the time while you visit the city?" The edge to my tone shocked me and seemed to surprise him as well, if his responding expression was anything to go by.

"I don't *need* you for anything, Kailiani. I want you. And I'm determined to have you."

"Oh," I whispered. "For how long?"

The waiter chose that moment to interrupt, bringing us several plates of food. Nero thanked him but never took his eyes off me, not even as the waiter said, "Bon appétite."

"Time is not something I'm accustomed to concerning myself with, Kailiani." Nero's irises seemed to ripple while he spoke, the blue hues swirling into the depths of his pupils and giving him a decidedly otherworldly air. It held me captive beside him, my breath catching in my throat. "You never answered my question. Why did you seek employment with JBI?"

"I… I need the money."

"Why?" he asked, tilting his head to the side. "To cover college debts? Living costs?"

"Yes." It wasn't a lie. It just wasn't the complete truth, either.

And somehow, he seemed to know, because his gaze narrowed. "I see." He broke the connection by facing the buffet of food laid out before us. "Perhaps one day you'll elaborate on that."

Not likely. "There's not much to tell."

"On the contrary, Kailiani. I think there's a lot more to you than meets the eye." He removed his arm. "Try to eat. I have plans for your body later, and you'll require the nourishment."

NERO

CHAPTER SIX

Kailiani was hiding something.

I could feel it with every fiber of my being, but I didn't know what set off my instincts. Maybe the way her nostrils had flared when she'd replied to my questions about her intentions, or the slight aroma of fear that had accompanied her less-than-candid replies.

She doesn't trust me.

Well, I supposed she hardly knew me. And it wasn't like she recognized the bond between our souls. Her human shell cloaked so much from her, even the siren within.

So, why did she need the money?

I knew of her debts, had reviewed them when I'd researched the background of her current life on Earth. But her finances weren't unmanageable. Of course, something had made her drop out of school early. I'd bet one of my seas on that being related.

She remained silent while I drove, her hands twisting in her lap. Our dinner conversation had become a bit stilted after her obvious deflection. However, she'd eaten, which was what I cared about most. Mortals were fragile, and I would not allow this one to break.

"What are you thinking about over there, little siren?" I asked while navigating the city traffic. Most would have hired a driver, but I preferred to indulge myself when in other realms, and this sexy little sports car met the mark. I definitely approved of this new technology period on Earth.

"Why me?" Her tone held a note of wonder in it. "Why a week? Are you here for work? For pleasure? Both? What will we do for seven days?" The dreamy quality in which she spoke suggested she'd been voicing her thoughts out loud without meaning to.

My lips curved. "So many questions. In summary, I'm here for a greater purpose, one that does include pleasure, yes. A week seemed a sufficient time to acquire what I need before moving forward. And as to why you, well, I think you'll find everything about my visit revolves around you."

She looked away from the glass to stare at my profile. "And what does all of that mean?"

"It means you and I are going to get to know each other very well over the next seven days, darling."

"Before moving forward," she added.

"Yes, assuming I've acquired what is needed." Namely, an explanation for how a siren's soul could be trapped inside a mortal form.

"I see. So this is temporary."

"My stay in New York City? Absolutely." I longed for the oceans of Mythios, for my beloved Aquaine Kingdom. What would Kailiani think of it? Would it provoke some of her soul's memories to surface? Or would it all appear brand new and overwhelming?

She fell into a thoughtful silence again.

"What's troubling you?" I wondered out loud, sensing her tension as I pulled into the underground garage beneath my current residence.

She shook her head. "It's… nothing."

Such a human reply. Well, if she didn't want to discuss her concerns, then we would engage our mouths in other, more productive ways.

I pulled up to the valet station and stepped out without a word, tossing my keys to the man waiting to park my car. Kailiani opened her own door—the impatient minx—and stood, her eyes full of questions. I dared her with a look to ask them, but she glanced down instead.

Fine.

She wanted to play the submissive siren tonight? Then that was what she would be.

I pressed my palm to her lower back, guiding her toward the waiting elevator. She remained pensive, her spine stiff beneath my touch.

Hmm, that wouldn't do at all.

I wanted her pliant. Begging. *Wet.*

A scan of my card sent the elevator upward. "The doors will open directly to the foyer of my penthouse." I skimmed my fingers up her spine to the back of her neck and wrapped my palm around her nape. "I think your dress will look lovely against the marble tiles, little siren." My thumb brushed her escalating pulse. "You'll disrobe for me as soon as the doors open. But leave the heels on."

"Y-yes, sir," she whispered, swallowing. "And my thong?"

My lips curled. "I'll take care of that myself, pet." Preferably with my teeth. Oh, but I wanted her mouth on me again. My cock hardened at the thought, eager to feel her wet tongue stroke me to climax once more.

The woman was a natural, thanks to her siren heritage.

Yes, we would start there.

Then, if she behaved, I would return the favor.

Bing. Kailiani shivered at the sound indicating our arrival, her pupils dilating with excitement. I definitely preferred this air of arousal from her to the nervous one she exuded before.

The metal parted, revealing the entryway and the floor-to-ceiling windows beyond.

I released her, allowing her to exit first.

She took a tentative step, her hands lifting to her dress, and paused just outside the elevator. Glancing back at me over one slender shoulder, she knocked the straps off her body and allowed the gown to pool at her feet in a puddle of crimson silk.

With a decidedly sexy shimmy of her hips, she moved forward, leaving the red fabric in her wake. I trailed after her, hypnotized and captivated by her alluring form. She possessed curves in all the right places, built for my hands to caress. Long, shapely legs. An ass that resembled feminine perfection.

"Take down your hair," I demanded, craving her soft, dark waves.

She kept her back to me as she slowly removed at least a dozen pins, each one taunting me by only loosening a curl here and there. But finally, all the strands cascaded around her in hypnotic ripples that I yearned to knot around my fist.

I came up behind her, my palms claiming her hips, my lips tasting the fine tendrils of her hair. "You're gorgeous, Kailiani. Whenever we're in my space, I want you naked. Just like this." I tore the lace from her sides, leaving her clad in only her stilettos. "Shoes optional," I clarified.

"Is that why I didn't need to pack any clothes?" she asked softly.

I grinned against the back of her head. "No, darling. I added that requirement because I already have a closet full of items for you." I bought them the other day while preparing for her to move in with me. While I wanted our stay on Earth to be short, I purchased enough clothes to last several months. Just in case.

"But you don't want me to wear anything." She turned, her midnight irises glowing in the low lighting of my penthouse. "Why bother with clothes?"

"Because I do plan to take you out, and as I've already told you, I don't share." I fisted her hair, yanking her to me. "You're mine, Kailiani. To dress or undress as I desire."

"A temporary toy," she mused.

"There's nothing temporary about it, little nymph," I whispered against her mouth. "I don't do interim arrangements." And the fact that she thought I could— particularly with her—infuriated me.

"What—"

"No." I started walking her backward down the marble corridor, toward the open entertaining section of the suite. "We're done talking," I continued. "The only thing I want that pretty little mouth of yours to do is suck my cock. Because while I enjoyed your ministrations earlier, I couldn't *see* you, and I want to rectify that."

Her eyes widened, her interest palpable.

"Yes," I praised. "I want you to look up at me just like that while you're taking me deep in your throat."

We reached the plush carpet of the living area, the back wall shrouded in windows that overlooked the Hudson. Oh, I would play tonight, both with my siren and the waters below. Something subtle. Just enough to sate the power rolling beneath my skin.

"Kneel, Kailiani."

Anticipation flooded the air as she licked her lips and gracefully fell to her knees before me. Her hands were already on my belt without me uttering a word, her compliance automatic and beautiful.

I marveled again at how perfect she was for me without any training. She knew exactly what I needed and how I desired it with minimal guidance. As if her soul—the one promised to me long ago—took over in these moments and drove her actions.

Although, it was that soul who'd betrayed me. So that couldn't be it at all.

No, this was all *her*.

Yet, they were one and the same.

So wonderfully confusing, providing me with a unique puzzle to solve.

She popped open my pants and slowly drew down the zipper, her gaze on mine the entire time—just as I'd requested.

And then she leaned forward to take me into her mouth.

Not lightly or gingerly, no.

But with the boldness of a woman confident in her task.

"Perfection," I breathed, grabbing a fistful of her hair to force her to take me deeper. And she did. Amazingly. Thoroughly. All while staring up at me with heat simmering in her alluring irises. "Spread your thighs." They were too close together—because my naughty vixen was trying to seek friction.

She complied on a mewl of displeasure, leaving a gap between her legs. The sound of protest went straight to my balls, making me want to do all manner of sordid things to her. Like make her scream while I fucked her throat.

"Use your hands on me, Kailiani. Give me everything." The yearning in her gaze intensified, one of her palms wrapping around my base while her opposite grabbed my sack.

"You look so beautiful on your knees." I brushed my knuckles over her cheek and tightened my grip in her hair with my other hand. "I'm going to fuck your mouth now, Kailiani. Try to remember to breathe."

Her pupils expanded, her lower body squirming.

"Don't close those legs," I warned, sensing what she wanted and refusing to allow her relief. Not yet, but soon.

My hips bucked toward her, my cock plunging between her lips. Her eyes widened, shocked, but I'd warned her. And being the good little siren that she was, she immediately accommodated by relaxing her throat to accept my thrusts.

"Flawless," I groaned, needing more. "Fuck, Kailiani." I'd never expected it to be like this with her—this whirlpool of intense passion that overrode thought.

A tear slid from her eye, my punishing pace a shock to her. Yet, she didn't shy away; she merely worked harder, sucking and licking and using her teeth to spur me on.

It was electrifying, calling to the energy within me to hum freely through my veins.

The Hudson outside answered, swirling to my command in the darkest bowels, away from human eyes, urging me to take charge.

But Kailiani's eyes held me captive.

Reminding me of what unleashing my power could do to her and her perceived home.

I harnessed the gift and used it in the sensuality of the moment, taking her mouth with a brutal force that only she could accept.

"Touch yourself," I demanded on a growl. "But don't you dare come, Kailiani." No, I wanted her to shatter beneath my authority, not her own.

She whimpered, the sound a vibration against my shaft,

as her hand dipped between her splayed thighs. Yearning swirled in those beautiful irises, darkening them to a near black. It sent my body into overdrive, showering me in a wave of euphoria that forced me over the cliff into the darkest kind of bliss.

I didn't give her the option to pull away this time.

No.

I wanted to see her swallow my essence to completion.

Her gaze smoldered as I erupted down her throat, her sensual mouth sucking and stroking in all the right ways. I shuddered, the force hitting me square in the gut.

Unnatural waves crashed against the shores of the Hudson in response to my undulating power, Kailiani's name a hiss on the wind.

So fucking good.

Even better than before.

It left me breathless. Crippled. *Hers.*

She owned me in that moment. Completely. Utterly. Forever.

I smoothed my palm down the back of her head, my subtle way of thanking her for the experience. Her eyes pleaded with me, tears prickling at their depth. She'd gone rigid, her hand clamped tightly between her legs.

Poor little one. She was waiting to come, her body strung tight with intense need. I pulled away from her mouth to kick off my pants, shoes, and socks. Then scooped her up into my arms to carry her to my room.

She trembled as I set her down on the soft mattress. "I'll take care of you, Kailiani," I promised, removing my jacket. "Spread those thighs for me, sweet siren. Let me see how ready you are."

Her creamy skin parted to reveal slick folds begging for my mouth. I removed my cuff links, then slowly unbuttoned my shirt while she fought not to squirm before my eyes.

"Tell me what you want, Kailiani," I encouraged, wanting to hear the breathy quality of her voice.

She didn't disappoint. "To come."

"Mmm." The fabric slid from my shoulders, falling to the floor. "You have such a pretty pussy, sweetheart." I knelt on the bed between her splayed legs and smiled as goose bumps pebbled along her limbs.

"Please, Nero," she begged. "Please let me come."

I leaned over to part her folds with my fingers and focused on the heart of her. "Poor little siren. You're so swollen. Does it hurt?"

"Yesss," she hissed, her hips undulating beneath my gaze. "I *need*…"

"I know," I whispered, bending to lick her tender nub. She screamed in reply, not from an orgasm but from the sensation.

"Nero," she cried. "Oh, God."

I smiled. "Yes, that would be me." I ran my tongue over her again. Tears slid freely from her eyes in response, her form nearly frozen from her beautiful restraint. I would be rewarding her for that. Right now. "I'm going to devour you until you beg me to stop, Kailiani. Come for me, darling, and don't hold back. I want to hear you scream."

I closed my mouth around her, eliciting exquisite sounds from her. My name rent the air in a cacophony of ecstasy as she unraveled in the most gorgeous display of pleasure. I pressed my palm to her lower belly, holding her in place while I consumed her essence and drove her right over the edge into a second orgasm with my tongue.

Oh, I wanted more. So much more. Sirens were notorious for their stamina. I wondered how far I could push her little human body.

And so I did.

I licked her to oblivion over and over, causing her to

shake and moan and whimper until she couldn't move from the onslaught of it all. Her drowsy gaze held mine, her body replete from enduring my sensual assault. I lost count of the number of times she fell apart.

"More?" I asked against her damp flesh.

"I… I…" Her hoarse voice made me grin against her. "Nero…" Her eyelids drifted closed, her limbs relaxed as she fell headfirst into her dreams.

I shifted over her, pressing a kiss to her forehead. "Sleep well, my darling siren." And she would, too. Because I had plans for her mind.

NERO

CHAPTER SEVEN

MORPHEUS ARRIVED JUST as I finished pouring myself a glass of wine.

"Impeccable timing, as always," I said by way of greeting and snagged a second glass for my oldest friend.

He fixed his suit jacket—far more elegant than my attire of sweatpants and a T-shirt—and glanced around the living area with interest. "When you requested my presence on Earth, I thought you were joking."

"I wasn't."

"Clearly." He wandered over to the floor-to-ceiling windows to peer down at the Hudson below. "The humans really have gone and fucked up this realm, haven't they?"

"Understatement." I joined him, handing him his wine and clinked my glass against his. "To old times."

"Indeed." He took a cautious sniff of the liquid before giving it a taste. "Well, this has at least improved."

"Not everything is a complete disaster," I agreed. "But I certainly do miss Mythios."

"Is that why you called me? Looking for a lift back?" His gold ring twinkled in the moonlight streaming in through the windows. It was an enchanted band that allowed him to traverse the realms without a Realm Dweller. Technically, the item was deemed illegal. But no one would dare remove something so precious from a god. If I knew the being who'd gifted him the trinket, I'd seek her out myself. Alas, Morpheus adored his secrets.

Which was precisely why I trusted him with this task.

"I need you to access Kailiani's memories," I said, cutting straight to the point. They were within her somewhere, and I wanted to know how she ended up in this state.

"Your errant siren?" Shock colored his tone. "I thought you intended to kill her, not complete the vows." His icy blue gaze took on a knowing gleam. "Has she tricked you, old friend?"

I snorted and canted my head toward the hallway. "Come. See for yourself." He'd be able to sense her soul's presence inside the mortal form, as it was linked to his gift.

Morpheus could control and manipulate matters of the mind. Specifically, dreams. But he could also access memories within dormant subjects. He often used them to inspire visual sequences while his subject slept.

I quietly pushed open the door to my bedroom. Kailiani slept soundly within my sheets, her luscious locks splayed across my pillows. Although I longed to join her, this was far more important.

Morpheus sipped his wine while eyeing her curiously,

power rippling around him as he accessed her mind. "Fascinating," he mused. "She's human."

I shut the door so as not to disturb her and replied, "I know."

"Her siren half appears quite content to remain locked away as well." He frowned. "How perplexing." He leaned against the wall, his glass to his lips.

We drank in silence for a long moment, mostly because I knew he was busy accessing her mind. It didn't take a genius to understand why I'd called him.

He shook his head after a minute and pushed away from the wall to return to the living area. "Someone has tampered with her essence," he finally said after taking a seat on one of the white couches. "She possesses memories from several lifetimes, all of which are woven together in an intricate puzzle." He paused, his gaze wary. "Her soul has purposely withdrawn to protect her mortal mind."

I sat across from him in a high-back chair. "What does that mean?"

"That some memories do not wish to be unleashed," he translated. "This won't be an easy favor, Nero. I assume you wish for her to remain unharmed?"

I didn't hesitate. "Yes."

"So you did complete the vows." He cocked his head to the side. "How?"

"Honestly, I have no idea." And had wondered the same thing when the bond had snapped together. It shouldn't have been possible in this realm. But I didn't regret it. Not even for a second. "She's not the woman who betrayed me, Morpheus."

"Well, the mortal, no. But her soul, yes." He finished his wine, set it to the side, and braced his elbows on his knees. "What is it you want me to find in her memories? The truth of that day? Or how she's been transformed into this state?"

"Both, if you can."

"Which is more important?" he asked. "Because if I press too deep, Rotanev, I risk her human mind."

I ran my free hand over my face, my other threatening to break the stem of my glass. "I need to know what happened to her," I finally decided aloud. "It's the only way I can help her."

"Help her?" he repeated. "As in, you want to release her soul? To make her whole again?"

"It's the only way to protect her."

He frowned. "I don't follow. As she's now bonded to you, she's automatically immortal. Albeit, a very fragile immortal who can be killed rather easily because of her human shell, but she's stopped aging. Right?"

I hadn't really considered that aspect of our vows, and while he was right, it still didn't fix things. "I don't want her to be fragile." Sirens were strong. They could fight. Humans... not so much. "If she is to be my proper queen, her soul needs to be free." It would strengthen her form, allow her to embrace all her natural gifts, her memories, her *purpose*.

His lips tilted upward. "How the tides have turned. Rotanev, yearning for his queen."

"She should have been mine several hundred years ago," I reminded him.

He lifted a shoulder. "True. But given her loyalty issues, perhaps it's best she wasn't."

A fair assessment. And irrelevant. "Will you help me or not?"

"It'll require staying in this realm a bit longer than I'd like, but yes, you know I will. And—"

"I'll owe you a favor in return," I finished for him. "I know."

He smiled. "I do like you, Rotanev."

"I know," I repeated. And the feeling was mutual. "Can you start tonight?"

"Yes. But it's going to take time to dig through her layers. I'll need her to remain unconscious for several hours."

"That shouldn't be a problem," I replied, smirking. "She's currently exhausted."

He arched a brow. "Something tells me I'll need her put in that *exhausted* state again a few times before I can find what you're searching for."

"Such a horrible task," I deadpanned.

"You're smitten." He relaxed into the chair and dragged his fingers through his blond hair. "Perhaps I'll find a human or two to enjoy during my stay. You know, to occupy my time throughout Kailiani's cognizant hours."

"I have an agency to recommend," I offered.

"An agency?"

"Yes. Of mortal females willing to do whatever you want in exchange for money."

"Money? As in human currency?" He chuckled. "How ridiculous."

"It's how I found Kailiani." Her photo had gone onto the internet—which was apparently one of the many places my Telchines had been monitoring. They'd recognized her face immediately.

"Interesting." His icy gaze burned into mine. "I wish to review this *agency* of yours, see if anything piques my fancy."

"It's not mine, but I'll get you the information. Just remember they're all human." Which meant he needed to proceed with caution, assuming he desired the mortal to live.

"I'll bear it in mind." His unreadable expression could be interpreted in so many ways. As I couldn't care less about his bedroom proclivities, I refrained from commenting.

"Can you start exploring her memories now?" I asked.

"Oh, I've already begun." His icy gaze glittered. "She's currently dreaming of you, Rotanev."

"Is she?" I rather liked the sound of that.

He nodded. "I daresay she's as smitten as you. Hopeful, too. But there's a darkness circling her. I'm following that strand. I'll let you know where it leads. For now, try to keep her asleep. And then tomorrow, exhaust her again."

I chuckled. "Gladly."

He stood and stretched. "Is there somewhere I can lie down while I work?"

"Yes." I showed him the guest room, down the hall from my master suite.

"This will do," he said, shrugging out of his jacket. "I promise to disappear when she wakes, but I'll be back around this time tomorrow."

"Thank you," I told him, meaning it.

"What are friends for if not to be engaged for favors?" he asked. "Oh, speaking of, don't forget the agency."

"I'll set it up for you tomorrow." I'd just have to call the Realm Dweller who'd helped me establish my alias here and tell him I needed one set up for a friend. Easy.

"Excellent." He collapsed onto the bed. "And, Rotanev?"

"Yes?"

"Maybe try taking her for a swim, see how her body reacts." He shrugged. "Just a suggestion."

I nodded. "Noted." It was a good idea. Maybe her inner siren would come out to play if surrounded by the element we both adored. "Consider it done."

He closed his eyes. "Enjoy."

With my Kailiani? "Always."

LIANI

CHAPTER EIGHT

IT WAS BECOMING INCREASINGLY difficult not to fall for Nero's charm.

I kept reminding myself that this was a job, not reality.

We weren't really dating.

Yet, this certainly seemed like a date with the way the sun beat down on my bare back while I sunbathed topless on Nero's yacht. He lounged beside me, his beautiful face turned upward, his eyes closed.

"I can feel you watching me," he murmured, his lips twitching. "See something you like, sweetheart?"

"Yes," I admitted. *A little too much.*

This was day three of our arrangement.

Just like the last two days, he'd floored me with having a

full itinerary of activities planned that didn't revolve around constant sex. Given the way we'd started, I'd expected to be fucked a lot this week. While, yes, that still occurred, he also spent time just being with me. Like a couple.

He glanced down at me, his ocean-blue eyes smoldering. "I like you, too."

My stomach clenched at the words, my heart fluttering stupidly in my chest. *Not real. Not real. Not real.*

Except, it felt very real.

I was so screwed—literally and figuratively.

I knew not to get attached, that this arrangement was temporary. He'd said so himself the other night when he'd commented on not staying in the city for long. It wasn't like he could just take me with him.

Although, he'd also said he didn't do "interim arrangements."

What did he mean by that?

No. Don't think too much into it.

We live in the real world, not a fantasy land.

But maybe for these next few days, I could play pretend. Forget Corban. Forget my worries. Just be myself and enjoy life with Nero, for however short it might be. These memories could fuel my dreams for decades to come. Something I definitely needed, if the last few nights were anything to go by.

I shook off the chill trickling up my spine and pushed the nightmares back into their box. They could haunt me at night, not during the day.

"Do you want to go for a swim?" Nero asked.

This appeared to be one of his favorite pastimes because everything we'd done this week involved water of some kind. Today, he'd flown us down to the Florida Keys on his private jet, just to take the yacht out for the day.

Yesterday was spent at the aquarium, where he'd rattled

off more facts about sea life than I knew existed. The man was a walking genius when it came to marine life. Which, I supposed, made sense considering his environmentally inclined occupation.

And the day before that, we'd walked hand in hand along the Hudson. At one point, he'd dared me to go for a swim. Given the March New York City temperatures and the fact that no one ever swam in the Hudson, I'd refused. But today?

"Yeah, I'd love to take a dip." I had craved the feel of the water since we boarded the yacht. He'd asked me on our date the other night if I liked the ocean. I did. But this was my first time being close enough to one I could actually jump into.

"Go on, then," he encouraged, waving his hand toward the back of the boat. There were stairs that led directly to the surface of the water.

I shivered in excitement. "Will you join me?"

"I want to watch you first," he murmured, his voice low and sexy.

Of course he wanted a show. All I had on was a thong bottom. I stood, happy to give him what he desired, and swayed my hips as I walked toward the edge. I leaned over just enough to admire the crystal-clear water below. We were too far out for me to see the bottom. The deep blue quality reminded me of Nero's eyes, making my heart skip a beat.

I had it bad.

Very, very bad.

But who could blame me? The man practically devoured me at every given moment, unleashed a passion within me I could hardly believe was even possible, and flew me to freaking Florida just to enjoy the sun for the day.

Talk about a dream life.

I shook my head, needing to clear my thoughts.

Best way to do that? Jump.

And so I did.

Bliss engulfed me from head to toe, causing a laugh to bubble out of my lungs as I surfaced in the smooth waves. I sculled my hands through the water to propel myself in a circle, loving the way my body seemed to control the essence around me.

Oh, I missed swimming. I used to visit the campus aquatic center a few times a week just to get a few laps in for exercise. An old coach once called me a natural. I just knew how to move through the water without thinking, my body automatically going through the motions as if I were walking.

Nero sauntered over in his swim trunks, his sunglasses hiding his gorgeous eyes. "Enjoying yourself?"

I whirled in response and tried to splash him, but he stood too far back.

A single eyebrow rose. "Are you trying to flirt with me, little siren?"

"Maybe." I allowed my legs to float upward, pushing onto my back and revealing my breasts to his view. "Is it working?"

He removed his bottoms, revealing his heavy arousal. "Maybe," he said, repeating my choice term.

The ocean seemed to part for him as he executed a perfect dive off the back of the yacht. He came up beside me with a shake of his head, sending water flying off his wild strands.

I shifted to my stomach, swimming along beside him with a few deft kicks of my legs.

"One might think this is your natural habitat, Kailiani," he murmured, moving with the expert ease of someone used to playing in the waves.

"You're not the first to say that to me," I admitted, picking up my pace for fun to see if he could keep up.

He did while effortlessly keeping his head above water like me. Not that we were truly racing. We were merely using our legs and hands to tread water on our sides. A little light exercise. And fun.

"A swim coach once tried to recruit me for a youth swimming team," I said, thinking back on the fond memory. "I'd spent most of that summer playing in the pool with my friend. The one you saw the other night, actually. It was my first time in the water—aside from baths and showers, I mean—but I picked up on it quickly. The coach I mentioned, well, he said I was a natural."

"So why didn't you join the team?" he asked, his gaze still hidden behind his glasses. I had no idea how he'd managed to keep those on his head when he'd entered the water, but his question weighed heavily on my mind, distracting me from pondering it further.

"My mother refused," I said, the memory darkening my thoughts.

"Why?"

"Money, mostly. She could barely afford to keep me fed, what with her, uh, habits." I really should not have gone down this path because it wasn't something I wanted to talk about. At all. "Anyway, I've always loved the water. I swam a bit while at college, but my aquatics membership expired when I disenrolled." Another topic I didn't want to discuss. "Uh, what about you? You seem to enjoy water."

Yes, good save, Liani, I chastised myself. *He won't see through that at all.*

"More than you know." His sensual tones reminded me of the smooth ocean surrounding us, all calm confidence underlined in palpable lethality. "Why did you withdraw from your university?"

Of course he wouldn't let that go. I sighed. Telling him the truth would only paint me in an even more inferior light.

But I didn't really have a great excuse, either. So I kept it vague. "For family reasons."

"What kind of family reasons?"

Oh, you know. My mother borrowed money from a loan shark—a lot of money—and then skipped town. "My mom needed my help with something."

"Something financially related?" he guessed.

A logical assumption, considering my employment choice. "Yes."

He pushed onto his back, folding his arms effortlessly behind his head as he used his legs to balance beside me. "Is my money helping?"

No sense in denying it. "Yes."

"Do you need more?" A soft question, one that seemed to still the water between us.

I swallowed. "Y-yes." It came out on a whisper, shame following in its wake. The very nature of our conversation proved the unrealistic undertones of our relationship.

He paid me to date him.

To fuck him.

To do whatever he desired.

But the fact of the matter was, I'd do all those things for free if I didn't need the funds. Nero Rotanev didn't need to buy a girlfriend. Was he a rough lover? Yes. Was he dominant? Also yes. However, both aspects pleased me to no end. And more importantly, I enjoyed *him*.

He remained quiet for a long moment, his feet lazily kicking him in a circle around me as if claiming his territory. "Will you tell me how much you need and why?" he finally asked.

"Why do you want to know?"

Nero righted himself in the water, facing me. "Because I need to know which battle of yours I'm helping you fight."

"Why would you help me at all?"

He tipped his head toward me, one of his hands finding my hip. "Because you're mine, Kailiani."

"For how long?" I asked softly, allowing him to draw me closer to him.

"Where I'm from, time is inconsequential." He brushed his lips over mine. "We think in terms of eternity, not days or weeks or months."

That didn't tell me anything—a common theme to his riddles. "I don't know if I can let you help me," I admitted. "I'm not... I've never relied on anyone other than myself."

"Then allow me to change your mind," he murmured, kissing me again. "Let me prove how reliable I can be."

My legs wove around his waist as he masterfully held us steady without so much as a ripple. *Magic*, I thought. *Nero is full of magic.*

An inane notion, but he continued to do things that surprised me.

Such as wanting to help me with my problems.

And keeping us buoyant without much effort.

If I didn't know better, I'd say he was standing on the bottom.

Stop thinking, I told myself. *Enjoy him. Enjoy this. Live in the moment.*

I ran my tongue along his lower lip. "I've always wanted to have sex in the water." The words came from me unbidden, the darkness in my core taking control of my mouth without permission. But the way his arousal hardened against me said he was up for the task.

"You can't distract me with sex, Kailiani," he replied softly, both of his hands on my hips. The thong bikini bottom disappeared with a snap of his wrists, leaving me bare against him. "However, I'll happily fuck you and then pick up this conversation again afterward."

"I like the sound of that." Not the discussion part, but the fucking part.

"Grab one of the stairs," he instructed.

I glanced over my shoulder, surprised to find the yacht right behind me. *How...?* The head of his cock nudged my entrance. *Oh, never mind.* I clutched one of the steps and arched into him. "I'm ready."

"I know," he replied, his mouth against mine. "Now hold on, my little water nymph. This is going to be rough."

NERO

CHAPTER NINE

KAILIANI's dark hair painted an alluring image across my pillows, her eyes dancing behind her closed lids. I longed to wake her, to hold her, to fuck her again, but she needed her rest.

And I needed answers.

We were on night seven of this arrangement where I exhausted her throughout the day and allowed Morpheus to work on her mind at night.

He stood in the doorway, his hands in the pockets of his dress pants, his gaze narrowed. "There's something in this strand," he said, his voice deep with exhaustion. "Something... that doesn't want to be found."

I didn't bother telling him to follow it. He had several millennia under his belt. He knew what he was doing.

Rather than interrupt his work, I stepped out of the room to fix myself another much-needed drink before retrieving my phone. JBI had sent me a message earlier asking if I wanted to extend my contract with Kailiani.

I didn't want to extend it.

I wanted to end it and keep her for eternity.

But I couldn't do that until I knew what secrets were locked inside her mind.

She very clearly had no idea who and what she really was, something she evidenced every time I took her swimming. Her natural talents showed in her movements, her confidence in the water rivaling a siren's, but she swam with the strokes of a human. No magic. No enchantment. No siren song.

It baffled me and infuriated me. Someone had done this to her, and I very much wanted to know *who*.

Had it been the price she paid to escape me?

Would discovering the truth unearth the siren locked inside her?

What would that discovery do to the female I'd entertained this week? Because I rather liked this version of Kailiani. She was subservient, sexy, intelligent, and very much *mine*.

I didn't want to lose that or her, but I also needed the siren to come out to play. That siren was her inner immortality, the being meant to remain by my side for eternity.

Shoving the questions to the back of my mind, I finished my drink and sent a message off to JBI about keeping Kailiani for a month. The sum I offered was one they wouldn't question. And if by some chance they did, I'd double it.

Satisfied, I set my phone on the counter just as Morpheus entered the kitchen with a blank expression. I arched a brow. "Find something?"

"Yes." His icy irises glimmered like silver beneath the low lighting of my kitchen. "I've been dancing through her memories all week, and I finally found the one you need."

I studied him. "Well?" I prompted when he didn't continue.

"I think it's best you view it through her mind."

Which meant he didn't want to be the messenger of bad news. "I see."

We stared at each other for another beat, then I led the way back to the bedroom. Kailiani remained asleep, her full lips parted on a sigh, her cheeks slightly flushed. "Doesn't seem to be a bad memory."

"Because she's currently dreaming of the last few days," he said. "Not the past."

I nodded, taking the chair beside the bed. As much as I hated to disturb her happiness, I needed to understand what had happened to her in order to help fix her. "Then let's revisit history, shall we?"

He dipped his chin in acknowledgment and leaned casually against the door frame.

"Try not to disturb the memory," he advised in a soft whisper meant for sleep. "And don't fight me."

I closed my eyes in response, opening my mind to allow him access. There were very few beings in existence that I would drop my guard around, Morpheus being among them.

It left me vulnerable to his power, a potential victim to his ability to manipulate dreams and call upon the past.

But that was entirely the point.

"Let her lead," he added, his words a hum of electricity against my thoughts. "Let her dream…"

LIANI

CHAPTER TEN

"HE'S GOING TO DESTROY HER," a feminine voice cautioned.

"You don't know that." The hissed response came from just outside the door, sending a tremor down my spine.

"On the contrary, I do. You forget that I've served him for over a century. I've had to clean up the bloody messes staining his walls. I know exactly what he's going to do to that poor girl."

I swallowed, knowing the woman in the hallway was talking about me and what Nero planned to do to me. This arrangement was written into my destiny long before my creation, leaving me with no choice but to accept my fate.

However, he seemed fair. Kind, even. Yet, the stories that kept reaching my ears spiked fear in my blood.

What if the rumors were true?

Would he ruin me?

Cast me to the waves?

Drown me over and over again?

He possessed the power of the seas, owned all of Aquaine Kingdom, and managed his creatures with an iron fist. If anyone could torment and hurt me, it would be him.

I shivered, listening intently for more, but the conversation had moved too far away. The knock that sounded seconds later told me why.

Sliding from my perch on the silky blue sheets, I landed on my bare feet and padded to the door. A man with golden ringlets as bright as the sun beamed down at me, his expression boasting a sincerity I felt to my very soul.

Dolos of Erebus Realm. One of the deities invited to tomorrow's ceremonial vows.

"Kailiani," he greeted me softly, brushing the back of his knuckles on my cheek in a gesture of respect.

"Dolos," I replied, curtsying low to demonstrate my subservience to his underlying power.

I'd immediately taken to the god after our introduction last week. His charisma and genuineness sang to me in a way unlike any other, and I found myself trusting him without really knowing him.

Unlike Nero.

No, I feared Nero and what he might do to me.

Although, I also hungered for him. Wondered what life with him would be like. Possessed secret hopes of a happy future.

Hopes that continued to dwindle as more and more words of his behavior reached me. Our courtship was typical for our positions and mostly founded on arrangements made long before my time.

I was created for him, after all.

He'd shown interest in me, had sent me gifts, even tried to engage in conversation a few times. But we both knew this arrangement was about merging kingdoms.

Trident, the father of all sirens, owed Nero a boon.

I was that boon.

A future queen meant to reign at Nero's side. Alas, all the commentary made it quite clear I would be serving from beneath instead of as an equal.

"What has you troubled?" he asked, stepping into my room with a frown.

"Oh, nothing. I'm fine." I shut the door behind him and turned. "Just… thinking."

"About tomorrow?"

"About life."

He nodded, a thoughtful look entering his emerald gaze. "You know, most intended brides boast an excited glow to them. Particularly the day before their vows. But you seem to be lacking that. Why?"

I sighed. "Am I that obvious?" Because I thought I was hiding it well. And in truth, I had been excited only weeks ago. It'd just been these last few days, living within Nero's realm, in his space, that caused anxiety to settle.

I knew the reason, of course.

All the little comments painting him in such a horrid light. If only he had time for me, I could ask him to explain. Although, one such recollection described what he did to those who questioned his reign.

So perhaps not.

"I'm just wondering how well I really know Nero," I admitted, sitting on my bed. "We were betrothed before my conception, so I grew up learning all about him. But meeting him is a very different experience." Mostly because I hadn't really *met him. He was too busy running his kingdom to spend much time with me, which I understood and respected. Or I was trying to, anyway.*

Dolos settled beside me, his lanky form much taller than my own. "I can imagine that's difficult for you to be promised without your consent."

"Oh, it's not that. I mean, well, yes, I suppose it is. But I don't mind the arrangement; I just wish I knew him better."

"Is it that, or do you wish you'd had a chance to live your own life prior to being committed to someone else for eternity?" he asked, his eyes

bright with knowledge and experience. "You're only nineteen, yes? An infant compared to Nero and the other gods of our age. He's lived for millennia, sowing his oats and refining his existence. While you were just created. Some may call that unfair."

I frowned, both at his words and his candor. No one dared discuss such things because they were just how arrangements were made in Mythios Realm. And to even consider otherwise was, well, reprehensible.

Yet, also interesting.

Because his comments held truth.

Why must I give away my innocence to a man I hardly knew? One everyone thought would destroy me rather than accept me as his queen? Was I nothing but a pawn for him after winning a game with Trident? That rumor—one I heard yesterday—hurt the most.

"She's just a trophy, one he'll use to his liking and kill once he tires of her. And the poor thing doesn't even know…"

The words still stung.

Everyone here had labeled me as naive, speaking ill of me without having even met me. All because they assumed their King of the Seas would destroy me.

Every word proved him to be a completely different god from my studies. Trident had called him just and considerate, a leader who truly cared about his people.

Well, his people disagreed.

"I didn't mean to upset you more," Dolos added quietly. "I just, well, I don't agree with what is happening here. Two people should be joined for more than just a consolation prize."

I flinched at his choice of words. Trident had told me Nero wanted me as his queen because of what he'd seen in my soul as it had formed in the cosmos, that he'd admired my power and beauty before he'd even met me. But it'd become increasingly clear to me that Trident had lied, that I was actually a gift to placate Nero, not someone he sincerely desired.

Which, of course, would lead to my eventual demise once he grew tired of his pretty little toy.

"I could help you," Dolos offered. "I mean, I know of a way."

I frowned. "What do you mean?"

"There are ways out of this arrangement, Kailiani. And that no one has told you of them says everything about the unfairness of it all." He sounded so disappointed, his features morphing into one of extreme pity.

I did not like that look.

And everyone kept gazing at me in that same sad manner.

I hated it.

Wanted to change it.

"Tell me," I demanded, needing him to know I wasn't nearly as weak as everyone proclaimed. I was a siren, destined queen of the waves. Not some breakable virgin toy for a god. I was created to be his equal for a reason.

Assuming Trident had told me the truth.

But why would he lie?

Why would—

"You could leave this realm," Dolos said, cutting off my thoughts. "There are many, many places for you to reside, kingdoms that would call you a queen. I can show you, if you like. I would just need your agreement to leave Mythios, then we could explore those worlds together, to provide you with a glimpse of alternate futures without anyone ever knowing."

I stared at him. "You would do that for me? A siren you barely know?"

He smiled. "It wouldn't just be for you, Kailiani. As I said, I don't agree with this arrangement."

"Why?"

"Oh, a long history." He relaxed back onto his elbows, his golden hair falling to the bed beneath him. "I could tell you more during our journey, if you like. But for our intents and purposes, just know I would not tell a soul about our travels. It would be our little secret and would grant you the opportunity of a lifetime."

My lips parted at the possibility. I knew of the other realms but had never considered visiting them. My duty was always here, to a god I thought I might one day love. Alas, his plans for me appeared to be unseemly.

A trip elsewhere could be the cure to my troubles, could provide me with insight to help my situation. Besides, it wasn't like Nero would miss me. His attentions were on his kingdom.

"I would be back in time for the ceremony?"

"If it's your wish," Dolos replied. "Yes."

I smiled. "I would very much enjoy a journey." An escape from all the cruel statements, conjectures, and fear. "Yes. Please take me with you."

He sat up, the sun bright in his features. "Truly?"

I nodded. "Yes."

He held out his hand. "I'll just need you to grant me access to your mind, for transport purposes."

A strange request, but as I'd never traversed the realms, I couldn't say what was normal or not. "I'm not sure how to do that," I admitted.

"Just repeat after me." He murmured an incantation that prickled along my skin, unsettling my stomach.

Black magic, some part of me instinctually whispered.

Yet, my lips were already reciting the words back to him as if pulled from my very soul.

I immediately felt light-headed, the world swimming around me in shades of blue and black. "Dolos," I whispered, clutching his hand.

His resulting chuckle held a note of cruelty that sent warning spikes down my spine. This didn't feel right. No, worse, it hurt. Like stabbing needles through my insides as my soul seemed to detach from my body, leaving me weak and broken on the bed. Only, Dolos lifted me into his arms, his touch cold. So, so cold.

"You're mine now, princess," he whispered, the words harsh inside my thoughts. "For always."

A jolt of terror rippled through my being, my soul understanding what my mind could not yet comprehend. Nero!

I shot upward, sweat soaking the sheets around me, eliciting a violent shiver. It'd all felt so real. Too real. As if I'd just dreamt of a memory from several lifetimes ago.

My eyes squeezed shut while I fought to regain control of my racing heart. If Nero woke up to me in this state, he'd worry, and I didn't want to do that to him. He'd kept pestering me about why I needed the money for Corban, promising to help me. While I wanted to let him, my pride refused. Somehow I knew if he caught me in this state, he wouldn't allow my deflections to suffice, and he'd demand explanations.

Which, of course, had nothing to do with my nightmare and everything to do with reality.

I only had one more day before the money was due. It was also, subsequently, my last day with Nero.

No wonder my mind had taken me on such a fucked-up trip. It was my stress roaring back with a vengeance after six days of ignoring all my troubles.

Well, I clearly could not ignore home anymore.

I scrubbed my hands over my face, wiping away the tears, and ran my fingers through my knotted hair.

Only then did I notice Nero sitting in the chair beside the bed, his arms on his knees, his intense focus on me.

He wore a pair of pajama pants and nothing else.

"I assume that's the information you needed?" The deep voice came from the doorway. I grabbed the sheets and tugged them up over my breasts in response, my eyes wide.

"Yes," Nero replied. "Thank you, Morpheus."

"Let me know when you go after him."

"I will."

The suit-clad male left with a nod, leaving me gaping after him in a mixture of confusion and shock. "Who the heck was that?"

"A very old friend," Nero said, his voice flat. "He dream-walks."

"He *what?*"

Nero picked up a glass and downed the contents, then stood. "We need to have a talk, little siren. About the man from your memory and what he's done to you."

"I… what?" Apparently, that was my new favorite word.

He sat beside me, his presence an automatic blanket of warmth that I craved despite the chaos rioting in my thoughts. "You studied mythology in college, yes?"

My brow puckered. How could he possibly know that?

"I reviewed your transcripts," he replied, whether because he'd read the question from my eyes or I'd spoken it aloud, I didn't know. "You took a mythology course just last year, which means you've learned all about the famous Poseidon."

Okay, maybe I'm still dreaming because what the hell? I pinched my side and flinched.

"I prefer Nero, but humans love their tales. They've called me Poseidon, Neptune, and several other names throughout history." He sighed, leaning back against the headboard. "And you, my darling Kailiani, are my lost betrothed."

I pinched myself again for good measure. Other than sending a pang up my side, nothing else happened. "Okay. This is a dream, right?" Because no way did Nero Rotanev just tell me he was Poseidon.

He studied me intently. "Look inside yourself, Kailiani. You'll see the truth of what I'm telling you. Just as you'll realize that dream you just endured wasn't a dream at all, but a memory of the day I lost you."

"You…" I trailed off. He couldn't mean…? "That… happened? Wait, you *saw* it?"

"Morpheus shared it with me, yes. He's been searching

all week for the cause of your current predicament and finally discovered it tonight in the form of Dolos." The name left his mouth like a curse. "I should have known."

"Dolos?" I repeated, picturing the familiar blond from my dreams. "No. I mean, yes, that's what he went by in my nightmare. But that's not who he actually is. This is all a misunderstanding. I'm stressed, so I fabricated this rather elaborate sequence in my head. Dreamt about it. Am still dreaming, obviously, since you claim to have *seen* my... Yeah. Okay. I just need to wake up now."

I tried to leave the bed, but Nero caught my hand and tugged me backward into his lap, his strong arms wrapping around me. "If he's not Dolos, then who is he to you?" he asked softly.

As this was all obviously not really happening, I decided to go with the truth. Because what could it hurt? He was in my head already anyway. "Corban, the loan shark who gave my mother a loan."

He stilled. "What?"

"Yeah, that's who I owe money to. My mother skipped town, tossing me up as her only collateral. If I don't pay Corban back, with interest, he's threatened to sell my body on the street, or worse. Since this all came up before I finished school, it left me without a bachelor's degree and a decent-paying job. That's why I joined JBI. If I'm going to prostitute myself, it'll be under my own terms." *Waking up right about now would be awesome, thanks.*

"And this—*Corban*—is here in the city?"

"Unfortunately," I muttered.

"You will take me to him." A demand, not a request.

"Sure. As soon as this sequence ends, we'll go." I couldn't help the sarcasm. As if I would ever let Nero meet Corban in real life.

"It wasn't a comment meant for negotiation. We will leave now so I can fix this."

"Fix what?" I asked, not following. Did he mean my financial problem?

"*You*," he replied. "He's done something to separate you from your true self, and I intend to make him fix it."

"Corban?" I shook my head, baffled. "I don't understand."

He released a long breath and pressed his forehead to mine. "You will, once I reunite you with your siren half. And then we will have a very long discussion about your opinion of me as a ruler. Because those whispers you heard? They were Dolos playing tricks. It's what he does. He's more famously known by the name Loki in your realm."

I blinked. "*Loki?*" I laughed—loudly. "You think Corban is Loki?" While I could somewhat see the similarities in the way he manipulated everyone around him, I definitely would not call the man a god.

"Every myth and legend you've ever heard is based on something real, Kailiani. Earth is the center between the realms, with portals that lead everywhere else in existence. It's why rumors are so prevalent on this plane. They sprout from a mortal seeing or hearing something they shouldn't, and rumors spread. It's how I became known as Poseidon. The Realm Dwellers try to keep our travels as concealed as possible, but mistakes happen."

Another giggle left me. "Right. Next you'll be telling me vampires and dragons are real. Oh, and elves, and fae, and—"

He pressed his finger to my lips. "Kailiani, all of those exist somewhere. I realize you think this is crazy, and all a dream, but it's very, very real. And once I've dealt with Dolos, you'll understand." He cupped my cheek, his blue eyes holding an intense emotion that stole my breath. "I will find a way to unleash your siren soul. You have my vow."

My siren soul.

Meaning he thought me to be an otherworldly creature as well.

No, more than that, he considered me his long-lost betrothed.

Making my vision a memory of the past.

Right.

Because all of that was perfectly logical.

I nodded.

Shook my head.

Nodded again.

Nope.

Yep.

Black dots decorated Nero's serious face. I'd forgotten to breathe. Couldn't remember how to now. Which was fine. In this world of make-believe, maybe I didn't need oxygen? No, I needed water. Because I was a siren.

I tried to laugh but had no air left in my lungs to manufacture the sound.

And wow, was I dizzy.

"Kailiani." The note of concern in Nero's voice barely registered.

His handsome features disappeared behind a cloak of darkness.

This was all too much.

Hopefully, when I woke, it'd be in a world I understood.

Although, a small part of me hoped I wouldn't. Because at least in this reality, Nero knew everything about me. No secrets there. Just… chaos.

NERO

CHAPTER ELEVEN

"THAT SEEMED TO GO WELL," Morpheus noted as I walked through the living area.

I snorted, ignoring his smart-ass commentary, and went to the refrigerator to retrieve a bottle of water. "Dolos is in the city," I told him.

"I heard," he replied, a tablet in his lap. "I'm searching for a Corban now, but I'm not well versed in this updated technology. I may need to call in a favor or two."

"Considering Kailiani thinks this is all a dream, that might be best." She wasn't in any condition to provide me with directions to the "loan shark's" house, but I wanted him dealt with as soon as possible.

That memory Morpheus had tapped into had set my blood on fire.

All those whispered words were a way to manipulate my innocent siren, and the demigod had succeeded. "I want to drown him," I seethed.

"I'll see what I can do about locating him," Morpheus replied, having his own reasons for wanting Dolos dead. The trickster god had a penchant for pissing off the higher deities.

I should never have allowed him to attend the ceremonies.

All this time, I'd thought Kailiani had played me by leaving the morning of our nuptials. However, no. It'd been the day before, and I hadn't even noticed.

Because I'd been too damn busy making sure all the gods played nice in my realm.

What I should have done was talk to my betrothed, to make sure she knew my true intentions for her.

Lesson learned.

That mistake would not happen again.

I found her sitting up in my bed when I returned, a blank look on her face. She blinked at me as I approached, visibly shaking herself from her thoughts. "Hi," she greeted me, her voice coming off a little too high.

"Kailiani, none of it was a dream," I told her, knowing that was exactly what she hoped. "Drink this." I handed her the water and sat beside her on the mattress. She didn't move or react, just clutched the bottle tightly. It gave me an idea.

Reaching over, I unscrewed the top and said, "Open your mouth."

"Wh—"

Using my elemental gift, I ordered the water to rise in a stream from the plastic to her parted lips.

Her eyes widened as she tried to move away from the substance, but I followed her with ease. "Drink, Kailiani."

"You can't—"

The liquid silenced her, slipping gently over her tongue. She swallowed because there was no other option, her alarmed gaze on mine the whole time. I only gave her a few sips, not wanting her to choke, and called the rest back to the bottle with a simple order from my mind. She gaped down at the item as if it had just bitten her, and set it to the side.

"As I said, humans call me Poseidon." A ridiculous name, but not all that much better than Neptune. "I'm a god by your standards, and you, darling, are my long-lost mate." I drew my thumb over her trembling bottom lip, pausing at the corner.

She needed to know everything, even if it meant repeating myself. It was the only way to break through her shell of silence, to prove to her the truth of our situation.

"Once upon a time, you were my destiny, Kailiani." She'd quite literally been created for me—a siren with the will of a goddess. "Alas, Dolos took you from me, causing me to believe you left of your own accord to spite me. I came to this realm to seek revenge, but what I found instead was a second chance."

She blinked several times, her expression shifting between disbelief and alarm.

"You're a siren, or you should be, anyway." I lifted my hand to run my fingers through her tangled strands.

She barely moved, but the slight flare of her nostrils confirmed she'd heard me, and she was breathing. A good sign for me to continue.

"Dolos—whom you call Corban—has done something to you. He's reincarnated you as human. When we slept together that first time, our souls married one another as was intended all those centuries ago, which means you'll no longer age. However, you're still very fragile in this shell. Rejoining your siren soul with your current form will solve that. But we need Dolos to tell us how."

And I would gleefully torture the information out of him.

"M-married?" she squeaked.

I chuckled. "Of everything I said, *that* is the word you choose to question?" I cupped her cheek, forcing her gaze up to mine. "Yes, Kailiani. Our souls have completed the vows. It's something that shouldn't be possible in this realm, but then again, our mating was written into the stars long ago. You are mine just as I am yours. For eternity."

Her pupils engulfed her eyes. "But I barely know you!"

"Your soul begs to differ."

"My *soul?*" She shook her head, dislodging my hand. "I... None of this... I mean... This can't... I'm not..." Words continued to fall from her lips, all of them jumbled and conveying broken thoughts as her mind processed everything I'd told her. I waited patiently, monitoring her breathing and heart rate throughout, and flinched when her palm cracked across my cheek.

"Oh, God!" She covered her mouth, her eyes wide. "I'm... I didn't..."

I loosened my jaw, the sting of her slap smarting. "I'm going to allow that only because I deserve a good punch for ignoring you the week leading up to our vows. I was so focused on ensuring the visiting deities didn't shred each other apart that I failed to check on what mattered most —*you*. All of this could have been avoided with a simple conversation."

She snorted a laugh that lacked humor. "Avoided..." Another laugh. Then she collapsed in a fit of hysterics that left me sighing beside her.

Yes, this was going to take a while.

When her giggles turned to tears, I pulled her into my lap and held her while she cried. I didn't know what else to do other than to offer her my strength. This couldn't be easy for her to understand, let alone accept. I understood that, and now, knowing how this all had happened, I felt very much to blame.

All this time, I'd thought she'd purposely tried to hurt me. While I'd tried to find her, it'd been for the wrong reasons.

She didn't deserve my wrath but deserved a heartfelt apology and centuries of groveling.

Dolos, however, would be punished. And far harsher than I'd ever planned for Kailiani. The demigod would drown for eternity.

"I'm being held by *Poseidon*," she whispered to herself. "A *god*."

"I prefer Nero," I reminded her. "Please."

She glanced up at me through her damp lashes. "Nero." Her uncertainty sliced my heart. I didn't want this lack of trust between us, not after everything we'd endured.

"I'm the same man you've gotten to know over the last week, with a few added responsibilities and gifts. But I think you'll find I've hidden nothing from you." Even while in the water off the coast of Florida, I'd held the waves at bay, allowing her a lagoon-like experience instead of a harsh, wavy one. "All I want is for us to finally have our peace, Kailiani. But to do that, I need your help in locating Dolos."

"Dolos," she repeated. "Corban."

"Yes."

She shook her head, then nodded, and then shook her head again. "I can't believe I'm... *this*... is happening." She pressed her palm to my cheek, ran her fingers through my hair, and dropped her gaze to my mouth. "You're a god."

"Yes."

"How old are you?" she marveled.

"Old. But as I told you, where I'm from, time is irrelevant. We think in terms much grander than years or centuries."

"Eternity," she whispered, clearly recalling my comment from the other day. "You kept saying all these things that didn't make sense, but now…"

I smiled, palmed her cheek, and used my thumb to trace the tear falling from her eye. "I never lied."

"No, you just evaded."

"Even then, not entirely."

She twisted her mouth to the side. "I suppose not. But you could have told me when we first met. Uh, again, I guess." Her brow crinkled. "Actually, did we ever meet before?"

"I didn't tell you because I thought you already knew. It didn't become clear to me until after I took your maidenhead that you had no idea of your true nature, nor mine. And as for meeting before, we did in passing, yes. But we were never afforded the time to speak like we've done this week. Which is now officially one of my biggest regrets."

"Why?"

Apparently, I'd not made myself clear earlier.

Time to rectify that.

"Because had I paid attention to you, none of this would have happened. I expected to experience thousands of years by your side and never once considered an alternative. So my entire focus had been on protecting my kingdom, not realizing that a demigod had swooped in right under my nose to steal one of the most precious beings from my life." I brushed my lips over hers, needing to reassure myself of her presence. "I'm sorry for failing you, Kailiani."

Her irises flickered, her nails curling into my bare chest. "I don't blame you."

"You should."

She shook her head. "From what you've told me, Corban —or Dolos, I suppose—is to blame." Her lips twitched. "I can't believe I just said that. It implies I'm starting to believe this madness."

"It's not madness."

"Oh, but it's definitely not normal, either."

"Depends on whom you talk to." Because in my world, it was very typical.

"Considering you're the first god I've ever met…" She trailed off, her pupils contracting. "Wait, Corban is a god, too?"

"A demigod, yes. Still powerful, but not quite as strong as a full deity like me and Morpheus."

"And I'm a siren."

"You possess the soul of one, yes. But you are very human."

"Right." She chewed her lower lip. "So that dream I had was real? All the stuff about Trident? The cosmos? Being created for you?"

I nodded. "All accurate."

"So, uh, what happens when you free my soul? Do I die?"

"No." An emphatic response because I refused to allow such a thing to happen. "You resemble your former self in every way, apart from your siren abilities and resilience. In theory, once your soul is unleashed, it will merge with your current form."

"In theory."

"Yes. This is why I need Dolos, to determine what he did so we can undo it—safely."

She swallowed, her naked body suddenly appearing even more fragile in my arms. Mostly because all the color had drained from her face. "I… Do I get a say in what happens?"

I canted my head, catching her dropping gaze with mine. "What do you mean, Kailiani?"

"Whatever voodoo magic you plan to perform to, you know, *unleash my soul*. Will I be involved in the decision to actually move forward? Will you tell me what's happening?"

"Of course," I replied, confused by her queries. "It's your body, Kailiani. I would never force you to do something you didn't want to do."

She arched a brow. "Are you sure about that?"

"Have I done something to make you think otherwise?" I demanded, affronted by the mere notion of forcing her to do anything against her will.

She considered, then slowly moved her head back and forth. "I guess not, no. You're just very, well, *in charge*."

My shoulders relaxed as understanding caressed my thoughts. "Yes, as is my due as King of the Seas. But I would never make you do something you didn't want to do, Kailiani."

"Well, technically, we *mated* without my permission."

"Is it something you don't want?" I countered, already knowing the answer. Her soul would never have bonded to mine if it wasn't a mutual agreement.

"It's something I don't really understand," she admitted softly. "But I'm not necessarily upset that it happened, no."

I feathered my lips over hers. "I will teach you, little siren. However, first, I need to deal with Dolos. Can you tell me where Corban is?"

"I can show you…"

"An address is all I need."

She shook her head. "No. I mean, yes, I have it. But no, I won't give it to you. I will *show* you because I'm coming with you."

My spine went rigid. "Kailiani—"

"Nero." The emotion in that single word had me refocusing on her face, giving her all of my attention. "If this demigod destroyed *my* life, then I have earned the right to confront him. I am going with you."

A dangerous request. But also a fair one.

She was right—she deserved to face her attacker, perhaps even needed to face him to begin the healing process. Because who knew what Dolos had truly done to her all these years?

"You will do as I say, and you will let me protect you," I told her, unwilling to negotiate those two demands. "You may no longer age, but you are still very fragile. And I will not risk your existence for vengeance."

"I no longer age?"

"Correct." *Oh, there is still so much she doesn't know.* "Because of our bond," I added before she could ask.

"So I'm immortal?"

"To an extent, yes. But you're still *human*. You can bleed. You can die."

"What happens if I die?"

"I don't know," I confessed. "What we've done is… unprecedented."

"I see." She pinched her mouth to the side and slowly bobbed her head. "I accept your terms. But I get to punch him."

I chuckled. "Oh, I'll let you do more than punch him, little siren."

Her eyes sparkled. "Really?"

"Yes. It would be my honor to watch you destroy him." I kissed her again, this time with intent. "In fact," I whispered against her mouth, "I think it would be excellent foreplay to watch you draw blood."

She gasped. "Nero…"

"Ah, my darling, there is still so much for you to learn about me." I licked her lower lip and adored the way she shuddered in a breath in response. "Mmm, how about we start with an introduction to how I deal justice?"

Kailiani shivered, her interest palpable. "Okay."

"Then let's get dressed. We have a demigod to drown."

LIANI

CHAPTER TWELVE

GODS ARE REAL.

Those three words kept repeating through my mind. Each time, I glanced at Nero. Then at Morpheus. One was a god of the seas, the other a god of dreams who could apparently tap into the memories of unconscious minds.

Both appeared normal, apart from their uncanny good looks and dominant personas. But they fit right in on the streets of New York City with their tailored suits and long strides.

The early sun rained down upon them just as it did everyone else. No bright golds or halos or mists of power. Only two men with faces carved from the heavens above. Or the cosmos. Or whatever they called it.

Did Nero even have a father? "Is Cronus real? What about Zeus?" I blurted out, eliciting a low laugh from Morpheus.

"I love the human tales," the dream walker mused. "It's Chaos they should fear, but you rarely hear about her in this realm."

Nero cut him a look. "The concept of Chaos is too difficult for humans to understand." He glanced down at me and gave my hand a squeeze. "And yes, Zeus and Cronus are real, but not in the same way as your textbooks describe them."

"Oh." I wanted to ask him to elaborate, but we were almost to Corban's building.

I still wasn't entirely convinced this was real. It all seemed too fantastical. But I sincerely questioned my brain's ability to manufacture such an elaborate dream. Between the memory, Nero's revelation about being Poseidon, and the golden-haired dream walker beside me, my mind was thoroughly blown. Add in Corban, also known as Dolos, to the mix, and yeah, this had to be happening.

Which brought me back to the words *Gods are real* as we reached our destination.

A chill slithered down my spine, causing me to shiver. "We're here," I whispered.

"Excellent." Morpheus tugged on the lapels of his jacket and glanced knowingly at Nero. "After you, Your Waterness."

Nero snorted. "Thanks, you jackass."

Their bickering, while mildly entertaining, did nothing to cool the unease growing inside me. If what Nero had said about Corban was true, then we were about to face a man—no, a *being*—who had tormented me for centuries. And I had no idea what I'd done to deserve such a fate, no idea how to even accept that history.

I stepped through the threshold, behind Nero, noting the familiar staff waiting on the lobby level. I'd already warned Nero that they worked for Corban and that more would be stationed on the upper levels.

"Good morning," Nero greeted them, his voice bored. "We have a meeting with Corban."

Two burly men stepped forward wearing matching expressions of doubt. "Name?" one of them asked.

"Irrelevant," Nero replied. "Because you'll be allowing us up to see him. Now."

"Is that right?" The bald man slid his jacket open in a suave manner to reveal his gun beneath. "I think you should reconsider."

Morpheus draped his arm over my shoulders, tugging me back a few steps. "Let's give him some room to perform, little dove," he whispered. His intimate touch should have been unnerving, but oddly, it lent me a bit of strength instead. Maybe because it indicated a manner of protection I wasn't expecting, one that rivaled Nero's presence.

Definitely friends, I thought, already lucidly aware of that fact. It'd been written in their easy camaraderie and in the fact that Morpheus had ventured to New York City to help Nero.

I wondered at their history as both of the bulky men fell to their knees. Three more appeared from the shadows, guns drawn, and almost immediately collapsed as Nero sighed. "Up to sixty percent of the human body is water, with the lungs being composed of over eighty percent. It makes your kind so very, very weak."

Gurgling sounds echoed through the lobby.

He's drowning them, I realized, a mixture of shock and awe swimming through my veins.

The one who showed off the pistol on his belt passed out

first, followed swiftly by goon number two. Then the three from the shadows joined their fate.

"This is why gods don't play on Earth," Nero said casually. "Mortals die so easily and quickly that it takes all the fun out of delivering punishment."

Morpheus released me with a warm chuckle. "Ah, but playing in their dreams affords me a bit more excitement because I can keep them alive as long as I desire."

Nero glanced at him. "Fair point. Would you like to handle the guards upstairs?"

"Already a work in progress," Morpheus replied, his grin wicked. "Just waiting on your cue to knock them out entirely."

"Brilliant." Nero nodded at the elevators toward the back. "Shall we? Before we're noticed?"

"Already handling that as well. The security guard on the other side of the lobby was about to ruin your fun by calling in the authorities. He's currently having a terrible nap. Same with his buddy down the hall over there." Morpheus gestured to the left. "I can wake him up if you prefer to suffocate him on his own fluids?"

"I wouldn't dare interrupt your fun, old friend." Nero sauntered toward me and brushed the back of his knuckles over my cheek. "You all right, little siren? You're a bit flushed."

Yeah, because I just watched you kill a bunch of men without so much as twitching a muscle. "I'm fine," I squeaked.

He gave me a knowing look. "You wanted an introduction to how I deliver justice, remember?"

I did. Which was why I nodded. But I hadn't expected him to be quite so *powerful.* A stupid assumption on my part, given *who* this man was in terms of my history books.

Poseidon.

King of the Seas.

A Greek god.

Roman, too.

Although, it wasn't the death that bothered me. I knew those men deserved their fates by working for a man like Corban, could easily surmise what they did on his behalf to people who failed to deliver on their debts.

No.

What bothered me was the tingle spreading inside me at watching Nero in his element. The warmth flooding my veins. The very *real* sensation of want stirring inside my abdomen.

Desiring a man in the throes of a kill was so very wrong.

Yet, my body reacted to his energy, to the seductive wave of power rolling off of him.

His ocean-blue eyes smoldered, his lips curling at whatever he saw in my own gaze. "I think she's impressed, Morpheus."

"It would appear that way." His friend wore a matching expression of amusement.

"Let's go, sweet siren." Nero reached for my hand and pulled me forward at his side while Morpheus trailed along behind us.

The elevator didn't light up when Nero pressed a button, causing Morpheus to snort and retreat back to the bodies. When he returned, he held a badge that he swiped to call the car.

"If I didn't know better, I would say you've spent some recent time on Earth, Morpheus," Nero commented casually.

"You're not the only one who calls me for favors, Nero."

"Intriguing" was all he said in reply.

Bing. The doors slid open, and Morpheus used the card again, selecting the floor I'd detailed for them earlier.

"Let the games begin," Morpheus declared ominously.

"Or end, as it were." Nero slid his free hand into the pocket of his pants. "Knock them all out, Morpheus."

"Happily."

I swallowed, my heart racing in my chest. Corban always put me on edge, his intimidating presence one that I felt every time he came near. And now was no different.

The first time I'd entered this building, it was with my mother under the guise of an internship. Alas, it was really her way of introducing me to her loan shark as potential collateral in exchange for more money.

Money she used to escape this city without me.

He'd phoned me a week later requesting a follow-up meeting, which I'd thought was to discuss a job because I hadn't learned his true identity yet. I'd learned the truth that afternoon: my mother had used me as a bargaining chip, and I now owed him tens of thousands of dollars. If I couldn't pay, he would find a useful way for me to work for him—on the street.

The memory scattered goose bumps down my arm just as we arrived at his familiar floor. Nero's grip tightened, but his stance remained otherwise casual. He led us into the marble interior, glancing left and right at the windows at the end of each hallway. The reception desk before us was vacant.

Actually, no. The receptionist was asleep on the floor. Same with the security guard at the mouth of the darker corridor that led to Corban's office.

I pointed toward it to tell Nero which way to go, but he was already moving in that direction. He released me, gesturing for me to walk behind him, and Morpheus took up the rear.

I have gods for bodyguards, I thought. *This is my life. Like, what the actual fuck?*

If it weren't for our surroundings, I might have laughed. Because all of this was ludicrous. Yet, as we entered Corban's office, his expression said it all.

No shock.

No curiosity.

Just pure, malicious enjoyment.

"Rotanev," he welcomed Nero, his grin wide. "And I see you brought Morpheus with you. Why, it's been several centuries, no?" He stood, his all-white suit giving him a falsely angelic gleam. "I honestly expected you a lot sooner, but apparently, my plan worked better than I could have anticipated." He winked at me with that last part, cementing all of this as fact.

Which I already knew.

I just hadn't wanted to fully accept it.

"I'm glad you're amused, Dolos. That's going to make this so much more fun." Nero released me and clasped his hands before him. "Now, do you plan to fight this? Because I would love a reason to drown you right here, in the sanctuary of this shithole you call an office."

Corban chuckled. "And ruin the endgame? Not a chance, Rotanev." He refocused his viridescent irises on me, a whisper of secrets swirling in their depths. "How did you find him?"

"I didn't," I replied, my voice stronger than I expected. "He found me."

"Interesting." He glanced at Nero. "How?"

"Not that I owe you a single ounce of an explanation, but her photo came up in a search," Nero added. "Technology has thoroughly improved in this realm."

"Ah, yes, I hadn't anticipated that when she joined JBI." He shrugged as if to say, *Oh well.* "It was far easier to torture her prior to this feminist age. Take the eighteen hundreds, for example. I gave her a horrible husband who whored her out to all his friends. He beat her, too. Such a fun reincarnation, until he took it a step too far and killed her." He sighed. "Mortals and their darker inclinations."

Nero said nothing while I stood frozen.

He did what *to me in a past life?*

"Oh, but it taught me a valuable lesson—not to leave her life in the hands of others. I chose to mold her in the next life by controlling her mother, which has proven the best method over these last few renditions." His resulting smile was cruel. "Your siren is used goods, Rotanev. And I do mean, *thoroughly* used. For this isn't the first lifetime where she had to whore herself out to appease me. I suppose, however, you could thank me. She's quite well trained as a result."

My stomach churned with his reveal. "How many lifetimes…?" The question came out on a whoosh of air, my voice trailing off as the world began to spin around me.

"This is version twenty-four. We had a few false starts in the beginning, where you died in infancy or at a very young age. Mortal bodies are so fragile. But your soul is immortal, allowing me to easily place you in new hosts."

"H-how?" I demanded, not understanding how any of this was possible.

"Quite simple, really. Find a fertile female, hook her up with a male, and thrust your soul inside their inevitable creation. The downsides are waiting the nine months for you to be born and, more recently, keeping you alive through childhood long enough to torment you. I mean, I had fun with your child mind in the beginning, but you broke far too easily. So in the recent two centuries, I started playing with you in your later adolescent years and, eventually, your adult lives."

I was going to be sick.

This man, thing, *demigod*, was a monster.

Part of me wanted to demand he tell me the things he'd done. The smarter part of me refused to know.

A child?

An infant?

Twenty-four different lives?

"Now, for my favorite part," he continued, refocusing on a very silent Nero. "Your bond may have stopped her from aging, but as you can see, she's still very human and can therefore die easily. And the only way to return her to her siren state is by forcing her soul to merge with her mind. Which would unleash all of her memories. Every horrible, vile thing that's been done to her, including men who have used and abused her body in the worst ways you can imagine, every death she's experienced, all the horrors inflicted on her child forms. Every. Single. Detail."

He paused, letting that sink in.

And it did.

Deep.

A tunnel had engulfed my vision, closing the room in around me, making it impossible to see Nero's reaction. But I felt his reassurance surrounding me, his energy rippling over my skin in calming strokes. It was all that kept me standing.

"So, now you have to choose. Would you like a fragile bride or a mentally weak one? Because I can guarantee you, Rotanev, the horrors she's experienced will *destroy* her if you force her to remember them all." Corban sounded so pleased with himself. Excited, even. While all I could do was focus on remembering how to breathe.

He'd damned me to an eternity of pain.

For what?

Why?

What had I done to him to deserve such a fate?

Oh, but the only way to know was to merge my soul with

my mind. How did I even begin to do that? Wait, no, he implied *Nero* had to do it by force.

Would he do that to me?

I shook my head, alarmed, confused, mortified. He'd said anything involving my body would be my choice. He wouldn't thrust that destiny upon me without my permission. Right?

An arm braced my lower back as my knees collapsed beneath me. "Take him to Mythios," Nero demanded. Gurgling sounds—coming from Corban, maybe?—mingled with Nero's words, causing them to muddle in my mind. "Keep him there for me until I return."

I had no idea whom he was talking to. Morpheus, perhaps? And what was Mythios? The place he was from? I sort of recalled that from my not-a-dream.

A shriek followed, the high-pitched frequency indicating pain.

But I couldn't see, couldn't focus beyond inhaling and exhaling.

I swallowed, the world swimming in shades of blue and black. Someone spoke, but I missed it, the rhythm in my ears too loud. It was reminiscent of a waterfall gushing over rocks, or how I imagined it would sound, anyway. I'd never actually seen one.

Or maybe I had.

In a past life.

Oh, God. I had all these generations, histories, that I knew nothing about. Horrible, terrible *memories*.

My equilibrium shifted, my head landing against a solid shoulder. *Nero.* His arms were around me, one beneath my knees, the other at my back. They reminded me of hot steel bands, warming my chilled form and providing me with a semblance of safety I craved.

This being owned me in the best way. I didn't need time

to know him. My heart already did, and I trusted him on an instinctual level.

He wouldn't hurt me.

Would never force me to harm myself.

No, he cherished me. I sensed it in my very soul—a soul I now knew to be a powerful being in herself.

A siren.

Forever trapped in a weaker form.

But maybe I could strengthen myself in other ways. Humans could be strong, too, right?

"Yes," a voice whispered against my ear.

Had I spoken the question out loud? I didn't know. Everything felt so fuzzy, overwhelming, a cloud of insanity hanging over my head. As if I were trying to navigate mist without a proper light.

That explained the dampness on my cheeks.

Or were those tears?

I sighed, relaxing into the pillow that was my Nero. I wanted to go home. To his home. Not in Mythios, but here, in New York. But maybe his real home, too. Wherever I would be safer.

No, I wanted my reality back. To not be lost in this muddled mess of thought. To *see* again.

The conviction gave me pause. If I desired to be a more powerful person, then I had to fight, not give up. Allowing myself to fall into this cocooned bliss of safety where I relied on Nero for everything was not the right solution, only the simpler one.

Choosing the easy path meant Corban—*Dolos*—won.

I refused to accept that.

He couldn't *win*.

My eyes flew open to find the familiar surroundings of Nero's bedroom. He sat in the chair beside the bed, his head in his hands.

For a brief second, I hoped this had all been a dream —*again*. But I knew better now.

And I knew what I had to do.

I sat up, my heart pounding in my chest. "Take me to Mythios."

NERO

Chapter Thirteen

TIME HAD ALWAYS BEEN a moot point. But these last two days had been pure hell while I waited for Kailiani to react in one way or another.

Aside from telling me to take her to Mythios, she'd remained nearly silent. Hadn't even spoken a word when the Realm Dweller showed up to escort us to the portal back to my realm.

She stood on the balcony of my home now, her gaze on the crystal-clear waters below. I found her here often, her arms folded across her chest, her silky navy dress blowing in the calming breeze.

The two moons of this world cast a luminescent glow over the waves and bathed her in a sea of gorgeous light.

I longed to run my fingers through her dark hair, to press my lips to her creamy skin, to hold her slender body against mine. Alas, I refused to push her. She needed space to make her decisions. And I would not allow my needs to drive her.

But I would remain a protective shadow at her back.

My kingdom wasn't dangerous, just different. And the people of my world were not used to human visitors.

Her safety meant everything to me. So much so that I'd already begun taking measures to protect her in this fragile state, should she choose to remain this way.

Dolos was confined to the deepest depths of my seas, drowning over and over again while awaiting his eventual fate. I intended to let him rot there for a few centuries first. Seemed fitting after what he'd done to my Kailiani. When she reached a stronger mental state—and a decision regarding her fate—I'd grant her the opportunity to torture him in whatever way she desired, for as long as she wanted.

She'd been a victim in all of this, a pawn used in Dolos's need for petty revenge. Demigods were not allowed to own property in any of the realms maintained by the gods. When he'd petitioned for a territory in Mythios two millennia ago, it'd been an easy request to vote against. The trickster had pretended not to care. His actions of late proved otherwise. And apparently, I'd been the unlucky target of his wrath, making Kailiani the victim of his cruel joke.

He would pay for what he'd done.

Miserably.

But first, I had to soothe my wounded heart—my Kailiani.

I leaned an elbow against the white railing of my palace, my loose pants fluttering from the wind coming off the ocean. "Can I get you anything?" I asked her softly.

She shook her head, not looking at me.

I sighed, retreating back to our bedroom.

We'd shared a bed these last two nights—fully clothed. Well, me without a shirt because that was my usual attire here. I spent a lot of time near or in the water, which made clothing a hindrance rather than a luxury.

"I can see where the Trojan and Greek myths come from," Kailiani said, her voice carrying to me on a breeze. "And some of the inspiration for current architecture in the Greek Islands. All you need are blue domes, and this could easily pass for Santorini. Not that I've been."

I'd moved toward her cautiously while she spoke, uncertain if her words were meant for me or for herself. But she faced me as I returned, her dark eyes clear and filled with conviction.

"It's very peaceful here, Nero."

"Yes," I agreed. "There are the occasional issues and territory breaches, but my people prefer tranquility. A common trait of the seas."

Her lips curled a little with the first smile I'd seen in what felt like a millennium. "I like it here, Nero."

A weight seemed to lift from my shoulders, one I hadn't realized I was carrying. There'd been this nagging worry that she might not approve of Mythios, that perhaps that was the real reason she'd left all those years ago. Which I knew was ridiculous, but this female created insecurities inside of me that I'd never known were possible.

I wanted her to like me. To like Mythios. To yearn to stay here in the Aquaine Kingdom. Whether it be in her human form or as a siren, I needed her to choose this willingly, not because she felt obligated to remain by my side.

"I like you here," I admitted, returning to the railing.

Another realization had occurred to me over the last few days—I'd been lonely without her. Yes, I had my people and my close lieutenants, but eternity without a mate created a very solitary existence. And I craved to have someone to share all of this with, a partner in the truest nature of the word.

"I sort of expected you to have a harem, or some kind of crazy party lifestyle," she continued, her lips twitching again. "You know, to match all the myths."

I snorted. "I've not attended a party in... a very long time." Not since the day of our pending nuptials, where my bride had never showed at the altar. And even then, it'd ended in disaster, not in entertainment. "There are some of my kind who do indulge in that lifestyle, but I've never preferred it. And as for a harem, no. I'm not innocent by any stretch of the imagination, but you are the only queen for me. I will not indulge any other."

Not just because of the vows, but because I would never desire anyone in the same manner as I did Kailiani.

Her eyebrows lifted. "Did you just...? Like, ever? Or temporarily?"

I was really starting to despise that word. "What about this feels temporary to you?"

"No, that's not what I meant. I'm, well, surprised. You just declared to always be faithful to me. I think." She shook her head as if to clear it. "I need to start this conversation over. It's not at all what I was planning to say."

And while I wanted to hear whatever she intended to tell me, I needed her to understand something first. "Then before you start over, know that I meant every word. And yes, I vow to be faithful to you. Always. You're mine, Kailiani. I have no wish or need for anyone but you."

Her lips parted, causing my dick to jump to attention.
Not. Now.

Yes, it'd been a few days, but I could wait years if that was what she needed from me.

"Always? For eternity?"

"It's not easy to kill a god, if that's what you're

wondering." I focused some of my mounting tension on the water below, creating a soft spiral meant to dance, not to destroy. "My soul is yours, Kailiani. Whether you want it or not."

"I do," she blurted out, her hand closing over my forearm and sending a shock of heat through my bloodstream. "That's what I was trying to tell you. I want to stay here. With you."

It took physical restraint not to pull her into my arms and kiss her. But I had to be sure I understood her first. "In Mythios?" I pressed, hoping that was what she meant by *here.*

"Yes. But as a human." Her expression took on a wary quality, as if she expected me to argue with her. And maybe a week ago, that would have been the case. However, knowing the cost of forcing her siren soul to emerge, I could respect her wishes. I also understood them.

"I've already begun enabling security measures that will protect you in your current state, just in case that was your decision."

Relief shone bright in her gaze. "Then you accept my choice?"

"Of course." This time I did give in to the urge to touch her and pressed my palm to the side of her face. "Just because our souls are mated does not mean I own you, Kailiani." Well, not in that respect, anyway. I did lay claim to her body and heart. And anyone who tried to take them from me would suffer a fate similar to Dolos's.

"There's something else," she whispered, leaning into my hand, her eyes warm. "I've thought a lot about this, but I'm to going live forever, right? In my current state? Like, I can't die unless I'm killed?"

I bristled at the thought. "No one will touch you." Not on my watch.

She smiled. "I know. I meant, that's the only way I can die, right?"

"Yes, you've stopped aging, and human disease and other ailments can no longer impact you." The only way for her to perish would be via a malicious act, which would never happen. Because I'd rarely leave her side. And whenever I did, one of my lieutenants would watch out for her.

I would not lose my Kailiani again.

"So, I'll live for hundreds of years," she translated.

"Millions," I corrected her. "For eternity, Kailiani."

She nodded. "Then my theory is viable."

"What theory?" I wondered aloud, frowning.

"Well, Dolos tortured me for three centuries, or thereabouts, right? The way I see it is, if I live that long, or longer, with all good experiences, won't they counteract the bad? Or at least make those horrible memories easier to live with?" Innocence caressed her words, underlined with hope.

Her idea held merit and was entirely possible, but knowing the things Dolos did to her—things he'd continued to brag to Morpheus about on their trip back to Mythios—I doubted a few centuries of happiness would be enough.

"How about this," I murmured, cradling her face between both my palms. "When you feel ready to welcome your siren home, with all her memories, you let me know and we'll discuss it more. But until then, I don't want you to feel pressured or to assume it's a fate you have to accept. Humans can be strong, too, with the right training. And you have a fantastic teacher standing before you willing to give you whatever tools you need to succeed."

I leaned in to brush my mouth over hers, aching for a taste of her.

"You're mine, Kailiani," I whispered. "And I will cherish you for always."

"I thought you didn't own me," she teased, nipping my lower lip.

"Perhaps not your decisions, no. But you? This body? Yes." My arm slid around her lower back while my opposite palm clasped her nape. "But you realize that you have just as much claim over me, right?"

She grasped my hips, her thumbs brushing the exposed skin along my sides. "Do I?"

"You do."

"I own a god?" She giggled, and the sound went straight to my heart.

"You own a king," I countered.

"Mmm." She tilted her head to the side, a devious twinkle entering her gaze. "Then will this king take his queen to bed? I'd like to make some waves."

I grinned. "Are you flirting with me, little siren?"

"No. I'm propositioning you, Your Highness."

"How much time do you require?" I asked, recalling our first night together.

She didn't miss a beat. "Ninety minutes ought to suffice."

"I think that can be arranged." I lifted her into my arms. "For our first round, anyway."

"Additional time will cost you additional money," she warned as I carried her into the bedroom.

"And what kind of currency would you like to exchange, Miss Mikos?"

Her lips curled. "Orgasms, Mister Rotanev."

"Ah." I pretended to think about it before tossing her onto the bed and crawling over her. "Well, fortunately, I'm well versed in that form of currency."

"Then I accept your terms," she whispered, her arms circling my neck.

"Good." I licked her lower lip. "Then prepare to scream,

darling siren. Because I've longed to hear you sing my name from our bed."

I kissed her soundly.

Completely.

Thoroughly.

Reaffirming our vows in the place they should have begun.

I expected to feel a hint of regret, a touch of guilt, but all I could do was smile. Because this was the way we were meant to be, and I wouldn't change a second of it for the world.

The best rewards were the ones we fought for, and Kailiani and I had fought harder than most. Which made us destined for one another.

Just as the cosmos had described.

Mates.

For the rest of time.

Thank you for reading Rotanev!

This story is one of the many rolling around in my head, and I can already see a dozen ways for it to continue. So I may one day come back to the Mythios Realm and continue exploring, as there are a lot of tales lurking among the various deities of the universe. I'd also really enjoy revisiting Liani and Nero to watch their relationship evolve.

However, I have some series to finish up first, then I'll consider going back to this world.

If you enjoyed *Rotanev* and want more, please consider leaving a review. That'll help encourage me to dive back into his deep waters ;)

Thank you, Cape Sounion - Temple of Poseidon, for inspiring this story. <3

Matt - Thank you for traveling with me to see the world and allowing my brain to wander.

Katie & Jean - Thank you for beta-reading and keeping Rotanev in line!

Bethany, thank you for editing. Rotanev still argues that it should always be "God" never "god."

Special thanks to 3DEA Editora for giving me a reason to pull this story from my head.

Thank you Uwe and Julie for the stunning cover!

Louise and Diane, thank you for keeping me above water when I'm drowning. :)

To all the readers, thank you for exploring this story with me. I hope you enjoyed Liani and Nero!

LEXI C FOSS

USA Today Bestselling Author Lexi C. Foss loves to play in dark worlds that bite. She lives in Chapel Hill, North Carolina, with her husband and their furry children. When not writing, she's busy crossing items off her travel bucket list or cuddling one of the critters in her house. She's quirky, consumes way too much coffee, and loves to swim.

Where to Find Lexi:
www.LexiCFoss.com

Cape Sounion - Temple of Poseidon

ALSO BY LEXI C. FOSS

Blood Alliance Series - Dystopian Paranormal

Chastely Bitten

Royally Bitten

Regally Bitten

Rebel Bitten

Kingly Bitten

Dynasty Bitten

Dark Provenance Series - Paranormal Romance

Heiress of Bael (FREE!)

Daughter of Death

Son of Chaos

Paramour of Sin

Princess of Bael

Elemental Fae Academy - Reverse Harem

Book One

Book Two

Book Three

Elemental Fae Holiday

Winter Fae Holiday

Hell Fae - Reverse Harem

Hell Fae Captive

Immortal Curse Series - Paranormal Romance

Book One: Blood Laws

Book Two: Forbidden Bonds

Book Three: Blood Heart

Book Four: Blood Bonds

Book Five: Angel Bonds

Book Six: Blood Seeker

Book Seven: Wicked Bonds

Immortal Curse World - Short Stories & Bonus Fun

Elder Bonds

Blood Burden

Mershano Empire Series - Contemporary Romance

Book One: The Prince's Game

Book Two: The Charmer's Gambit

Book Three: The Rebel's Redemption

Midnight Fae Academy - Reverse Harem

Ella's Masquerade

Book One

Book Two

Book Three

Book Four

Noir Reformatory - Ménage Paranormal Romance

The Beginning

First Offense

Second Offense

Underworld Royals Series - Dark Paranormal Romance

Happily Ever Crowned

Happily Ever Bitten

X-Clan Series - Dystopian Paranormal

Andorra Sector

X-Clan: The Experiment

Winter's Arrow

Bariloche Sector

Vampire Dynasty - Dark Paranormal

Violet Slays

Sapphire Slays

Crossed Fates

First Bite of Revenge

Other Books

Scarlet Mark - Standalone Romantic Suspense

Carnage Island - Standalone Reverse Harem Romance

Made in the USA
Middletown, DE
30 October 2021

51315815R00092